The Incredible Journey of Lacey Starr and Mabel Brown

Perry Dantes

First Edition

NEWMAN SPRINGS PUBLISHING
320 Broad Street
Red Bank, NJ 07701

First originally published by Newman Springs Publishing 2022

ISBN 978-1-68498-576-0 (Paperback)
ISBN 978-1-68498-577-7 (Digital)

Printed in the United States of America

To Joanna

Lacey and Mabel

The year was 1933. Lacey Starr, who lived in Mequon, Wisconsin, a suburb of the city of Milwaukee, dreamed of one day becoming a singer. In the Native American Ojibwe language, *Mequon* means "ladle," referring to the course of the long, winding river in the area.

Lacey was loved very much by her parents. Her mother was a homemaker and her father an engineer working for the Wisconsin Gas Co., a public utility company. At just twenty-one years old, Lacey had a beautiful singing voice. She always wanted to take her talents to New York City, but her mother was very much against the idea. "Why leave a beautiful state like Wisconsin with all of its forests and lakes for the concrete jungle of New York?" she said.

Although the state of Minnesota's motto is "the land of ten thousand lakes," Lacey's mom once won a bet by knowing that Wisconsin had 15,000 lakes. While Lacey fondly remembered family trips as a child to beautiful Beaver Lake in Dodge County, she knew why she always wanted to go to New York: the opportunity for a career in show business. She felt that New York was the only place she could truly fulfill her dreams.

With a last name like Starr, she thought her future as a singer was divinely preordained. Lacey majored in voice at the University of Wisconsin in Madison, Wisconsin's capital. She had a good Midwestern upbringing and education.

One hundred miles from Mequon, Mabel Brown—Black, pretty, talented like Lacey, and twenty-two years old—was living on Chicago's Southside with her mother. She also dreamed of becoming a star in New York's entertainment industry. Although she struggled financially, Mabel's mother made sure that Mabel received a good education. Mabel attended the University of Illinois in Chicago, majoring in both dance and voice.

One day, Mabel boarded the Greyhound bus heading for New York City. One of the few open seats was next to Lacey, who had boarded earlier in Milwaukee. It was nice to have someone to talk to on the long trip to New York.

During their trip, Lacey and Mabel were enchanted by views of the beautiful countryside. They started chatting.

"Do you know anyone in New York?" Lacey asked Mabel.

"My mother's sister lives in Harlem," Mabel replied. "And you?"

"I'm visiting my friend, Nancy, who lives in Brooklyn on 54th Street," Lacey answered.

"My aunt lives on West 135th Street near the Harlem Hospital Center. She is a nurse," Mabel said.

"You too want to be a nurse?"

"Oh no, I'm a singer and a dancer."

"Really? Me too."

"So we'll shoot for the same star. We must get together in New York."

Before they reached New York's Greyhound Depot, Lacey and Mabel had become good friends. After resting for a few days, Lacey and Mabel decided to go for a walk around New York. They took in all the breathtaking views and sights of the city. Although Lacey recalled her mother's opinion of New York (only skyscrapers and concrete), after they had passed St. Patrick's Cathedral, Park Avenue, Central Park and Broadway, and, finally, Madison and Fifth Avenues (the richest and most attractive shopping districts in the United States), both had become enchanted with New York.

Quickly, both girls from the Midwest realized that New York had become America's capital of finance, industry, architecture, publishing, theater, music, advertising, and fashion. Everything seemed to revolve around this city.

Lacey and Mabel didn't forget why they came to New York. Working in the entertainment industry was their dream. Let's face it—most big names in the industry came from New York: George Gershwin, Irving Berlin among the others. One of the first music meccas they visited in the city was Harlem's Cotton Club where the great Duke Ellington played. Mabel reminded Lacey that Duke Ellington was named "The King of Jazz" in America.

At first, Lacey and Mabel looked for jobs separately, but later, they went everywhere together. Having been a dance major, Mabel was obsessed with Florenz Ziegfeld's Follies. She read about his productions in the newspapers any chance she could get. For instance, she learned that while on tournee in Europe, Ziegfeld found his singing sensation, singer Anna Held.

Ziegfeld advertised her as French-born, but actually her name was Helene Anna Held. She was born in Warsaw and was the daughter of Jewish-Polish parents. She had a nice voice and sang songs like "Won't You Come and Play with Me?" or Irving Berlin's "A Pretty Girl Is Like a Melody." Some of her favorite lyrics from Berlin's song were:

A pretty girl is like a melody that haunts you night and day,
Just like the strain of haunting refrain,
She'll start upon a marathon
And run around your brain.

Although Ziegfeld later married Anna, there were rumors around New York about his infidelity. Ziegfeld's Follies was a big undertaking. He even featured many different wild animals in his show.

Born in Chicago, Florenz Ziegfeld made many people stars: Charlie Chaplin, May West, Ginger Rogers, Ed Wynn, W.C. Fields, Fred Astaire, Fanny Brice, Bert Lahr, and many others.

In fact, the Follies was Anna Held's idea based on the famous Folies Bergère in Paris.

Mabel dreamed of joining the Follies. Unfortunately, at that time, only White girls were hired for the show; Mabel was disappointed and heartbroken. However, both girls never stopped chasing their dreams. They waited for a break, and it came unexpectedly.

A very interesting and charismatic man lived a floor below Nancy's apartment on 54th Street in Brooklyn. His name was Aaron

Glickman. According to Nancy, Aaron was a stage manager at the 200 Club on West 52nd Street. When Nancy visited the club a couple times in the past, she had seen him working. The 200 Club was a classy place with top-shelf entertainment.

Nancy decided to invite Aaron for a chat about whether he might hire the girls. The possibility of working at the club got them very excited. He was to arrive at 8:00 p.m. It was already 8:15, and the girls were getting nervous. Finally, at 8:30, there was a knock at the door. Nancy rushed to the door to let the very handsome Aaron Glickman in.

"Sorry, I'm late. I was coming from Poland, but I was held up there," he said.

"From Poland?" Mabel asked with her mouth open.

"From Poland, New York. I was visiting a friend," Aaron Glickman explained. Of course, there was a small town called Poland just north of New York City.

"Some of my neighbors rumored that you were born in Warsaw, Chopin's birthplace. Is this true?" Nancy asked.

"Yes, I was born there. I'm a Jewish immigrant. Four million other Jews still live in Poland's Diaspora. They lived there for twelve hundred years. We Jews always remember where we were born. The word Poland or *Polin* in Hebrew means 'The Rest Place.'"

The girls were very interested in what Aaron had to say, but Nancy gently interrupted to introduce Lacey and Mabel to Aaron.

"I want you to meet my two friends from the Midwest. They came to New York to sing and dance. Lacey has a beautiful voice. I've seen you before at the 200 Club and hoped you might give them a chance," Nancy said nervously.

"Then you came to the right person. I'm the stage manager there. The club is owned by Sam Rothstein. He is a good man. It's not easy to run a club. There are so many risks."

"Would you give Lacey a chance?" Nancy continued.

"Let me think about it. In a month, we'll be hosting a singing festival of Bing Crosby's songs. Would you like to try?" Aaron asked Lacey.

"Of course. Thank you, sir," Lacey replied with a big smile.

"I'll stop by tomorrow to confirm which song you'd like to sing?" Aaron asked before he left. Nancy had learned from the other residents in the building that Aaron was a very intelligent and pleasant man. He was also a very hard worker. Aside from working at the 200 Club, he enhanced his income by teaching in the yeshiva in Brooklyn. Nancy also learned that he helped many newcomers on the stage.

The next day, Aaron returned to Nancy's apartment with a Bing Crosby song he thought would be perfect for Lacey to sing. It was "Just One More Chance," a beautiful song with Arthur Johnson's music and lyrics by Sam Coslow. The refrain lyrics went like this:

Just one more chance
To prove it's you alone I care for
Each night I say a little prayer for
Just one more chance.

Because Aaron recalled that the Polish version of this song was "Nikt Tylko Ty," meaning "No One but You" in English, he asked Lacey to try this version instead for the first refrain:

No one but you
To prove it's you alone I care for
Each night I say a little prayer for
No one but you.

He instructed her to sing the rest of the song in its Polish version. Why? Well, maybe because the song brought up fond memories from his old country, Poland, or maybe he left someone there that he deeply cared for. No one asked him why. He also didn't mention anything specific, keeping the secret to himself.

This song was perfect for Lacey's voice. She became an overnight success. Every night, fans jammed into the 200 Club. Were the song's new lyrics the reason for success? Was it Aaron's luck or his knowledge of how to best present the song? Or was it just Lacey's beautiful voice? No one knew. It was an unusual and remarkable phenomenon.

Lacey Starr won first place in Bing Crosby's Song Festival and became a star overnight. Her voice was perfect for the song. She became so popular that some Broadway agents even started to inquire about her.

Sam Rothstein, owner of the 200 Club, was elated. Big money kept coming in for weeks. Aaron Glickman himself got a big raise, and Lacey got her first check. Yet Aaron felt uneasy. He also wanted to get Mabel more involved with music and started brainstorming a couple songs for her to sing. Finally, Aaron shouted, "I've got it, Mabel!" He asked Mabel to start practicing three hits: "Georgia on My Mind" with music by Hoagy Carmichael and lyrics by Stuart Gorrell; "Body and Soul" with music by Johnny Green and lyrics by Edward Heyman, Robert Sour, and Frank Eyton; and "I Got Rhythm" with music by George Gershwin and lyrics by Ira Gershwin.

According to Aaron, Mabel had done a great job with these three songs. "I Got Rhythm" became especially popular with the 200 Club audiences.

So many great songs came out in the 1930s that Aaron was puzzled which ones to choose for Lacey. Out of five songs, he finally chose two for her: "What Is This Thing Called Love?" with music and lyrics by Cole Porter, and "Embraceable You," music by George Gershwin and lyrics by Ira Gershwin.

For a few weeks, both girls had become overworked and overexposed. Show business took its toll on the singers, so Lacey and Mabel decided to take a well-deserved break. Aaron was a very understanding man. While speaking to Sam Rothstein about the girls, he learned that Sam was invited to a large party attended by all of New York's celebrities. Sam couldn't go, so he asked Aaron to take his place.

Aaron accepted Sam's invitation, but he also knew that such an event would be a great opportunity for both Lacey and Mabel to learn more about the city's entertainment scene. He asked if they wanted to join him. Their answer was, "What should we wear?"

They felt they had no appropriate clothes for such an event. Aaron took them shopping at Macy's where they found dresses that made them feel chic and elegant. They were ready to tackle their first New York party.

The party was at the Astor Hotel. All of the surrounding elegance dazzled the two singers from the Midwest. Upon meeting one of the most elite members of New York's social scene, Adam Gimbel, Saks Fifth Avenue president, Lacey learned that he was born in Milwaukee and wouldn't let him go without asking thousands of questions.

Mabel, however, was more interested in Helena Rubinstein, a cosmetics giant. Mabel was so impressed with Helena after learning about her life story. Helena was born in Krakow, Poland. Mabel couldn't stop thinking about how much Helena accomplished as a cosmetics entrepreneur, having not even been born in the United States. So Mabel living in the greatest city in the greatest country in the world gave her hope that she would also have a chance to realize her dreams.

Lacey also met some other interesting people, the founder of the NBC television network, David Sarnoff and Anne Vanderbilt, a philanthropist who was born in Manhattan.

Aaron was moving through the crowd of people gathered at the party, and he ran into his old friend, Szymon Bizon, also an immigrant from Poland. His mother was Jewish and his father was Polish. Aaron met him on the same ship crossing the Atlantic when they left Poland for New York. Aaron liked him very much, for they were the same age, and both had similar interests.

Szymon didn't come from Warsaw but from Bialystok, a city in northeast Poland. Bialystok's population mostly spoke in Yiddish.

After the party was over and forgotten, Christmas was quickly approaching. Being a resourceful man, Aaron was able to get tickets to see percussionist Gene Krupa playing on Broadway with clarinetist Benny Goodman who usually played at the Waldorf Astoria Hotel. He was happy to invite Szymon, Lacey, and Mabel to join him to enjoy some good music. When Szymon found out that the Glen Miller band was playing at a Christmas show in New Rochelle, New York, all four of them decided to go there.

Aaron prepared his car for the trip, and they left for New Rochelle with Aaron driving.

On the way back, Aaron made a sudden stop. Everyone's bodies shot forward. Both girls were terrified.

"What are you doing?" Szymon asked.

"A squirrel was crossing the road in front of the car. I always stop for squirrels," Aaron muttered.

"You what?" asked Szymon.

"I'll tell you why. While living in Poland, I liked squirrels. They are beautiful animals. I watched them playing in the park. I fed them. I named one of them Basia, diminutively from the name Barbara. Although I must admit, sometimes, they remind me of rats," said Aaron.

"Did you know some woman named Barbara in Poland?" Lacey asked.

"I knew a few Barbaras, but I wouldn't get involved because my only dream was to come to America, and I didn't want to leave someone with a broken heart back in Poland," Aaron explained.

Lacey and Mabel found Aaron very secretive for not wanting to reveal his feelings for some woman or acquaintance close to him back in Poland.

At home, Aaron worked on the Christmas repertoire for Lacey and Mabel with help from Szymon.

"I've got it, Szymon," Aaron shouted. "Just like our country, the United States, Black and White. I want Lacey and Mabel to sing together," said Aaron.

"You are forgetting the Asians. They are here too. Personally, I prefer a mix of Black and Asian," Szymon said with a grin.

After Szymon's comment, Aaron wouldn't bring race or sex into the conversation. He suspected that Lacey and Mabel didn't have any experience in this field.

"You said they should sing together, but which songs?"

After a while, Szymon picked the proper song. It was a German song, "Bei Mir Bist du Schoen," with music by Sholom Secunda and lyrics by Sammy Cahn and Saul Chaplin composed in 1932. The English title was "To Me, You Are Beautiful." He started to sing:

Bei Mir Bist Du Schoen, please let me explain
Bei Mir Bist Du Schoen means you are grand
Bei Mir Bist Du Schoen, again I'll explain
It means you're the fairest in the land.

After a few rehearsals, Lacey and Mabel became a hit again.

Because it was originally a Yiddish song with the title "Bei Mir Bistu Shein," Aaron instructed the girls to sing the Yiddish version.

Lacey and Mabel sang this song in the 200 Club during the Christmas season and for the big New Year's Eve celebration to packed audiences. Sam Rothstein and Aaron Glickman were very content with their success.

New York, 1933

By 1933, New York was a cultural melting pot. With growing global prominence, soaring immigration, success on Wall Street, and new construction all over the city, New York had surpassed London as the cultural and financial capital of the world. Even the skyscraper was an American original—the first was built in New York in the nineteenth century. Neighborhoods like Harlem and Chinatown even permitted visitors to experiment with all their fantasies, including sex or drugs.

This fascination with New York was a phenomenon specific to the twentieth century. Why? An Italian resident of New York had very different opinions about his city than a Jewish one, although they both lived close by.

In 1933, there were approximately seven million inhabitants across New York's five boroughs: Bronx, Brooklyn, Queens, Staten Island, and Manhattan. Most people were from foreign countries or had arrived from other states.

New York had also become a city with a large Jewish population—about 40 percent were Jewish. The Irish population had dropped to 31 percent, and there were also sizable percentages of Italian and Polish residents. The Lower East Side was predominantly Jewish from Eastern Europe, especially from Poland.

Great New York aristocrats like the Astors, Du Ponts, Carnegies, Goodmans, Gimbels, Morgans, Rockefellers, Vanderbilts, or Rubinsteins were living in Manhattan. Lacey could easily blend in with a group like this if she could just have their money.

There were also gangs in New York. There were vendettas of the Mafia, Black Hand, or La Cosa Nostra. Most of the victims of the Italian gangs were found with their tongues split in the traditional

Sicilian fashion. There were Harlem's "Little Italy" gangs in the vicinity of East 125th Street. These were ordinary gang operations, but the majority of killings were the result of old reckonings from Sicily. And there was the famous Meyer Lansky, a Jewish immigrant from Poland, known as the Mob's accountant. Lansky was instrumental in the development of the National Crime Syndicate in the United States.

Great Gotham, as New Yorkers called their town, also had its problems: sewage, energy, garbage, etc. While the city had seven million residents, it had fifty million rats. The five boroughs were constantly fighting rat infestation.

And whose job was it to catch and destroy all the rats? Who had the dirtiest and most difficult jobs in New York? Usually Black Americans or Irish, Italian, and Polish immigrants.

Prohibition was lifted on December 3, 1933, and New Yorkers could now drink alcohol freely again. Lacey and Mabel were not drinkers, so when they weren't performing on stage, they tried learning more about New York's history. They loved exploring the halls of the New York Society Library and learning more about the city they hoped to make their home.

Grandezza Stella

When 1934 arrived, the carnival season continued. Because Prohibition was lifted, liquor was everywhere. New Yorkers were out on the streets enjoying themselves to the fullest. There were parties in hotels, masquerade parties at taverns, and private parties at homes.

The year 1934 was a turning point in the Great Depression in America, with unemployment decreasing to 22 percent. At this time, the average cost of a new house was $5,970, monthly rent was $20, and the average hourly wage was $1.60. The major news stories dominating the papers were about the rise of dictators like Stalin and Mao Tse-tung, the Oklahoma dust bowl that destroyed thirty-five million acres of farmland, and the FBI ending the careers of John Dillinger, Bonnie Parker and Clyde Barrow (known as Bonnie and Clyde), Pretty Boy Floyd, and Baby Face Nelson.

The famous St. Regis Hotel in the Bahamas invited Lacey and Mabel to perform for New Year's Eve, but for obvious reasons, they had to refuse. They were already scheduled to perform at the 200 Club. But not everything was lost.

The February blizzard of 1934 brought the worst cold of the century to New York. Aaron took it upon himself to organize a trip to the Bahamas for Lacey and Mabel to perform and get away from the cold. He instructed Szymon and the girls to get their passports in order.

The elegant St. Regis Hotel impressed everyone, and its beautiful concert venue was top-notch. After singing their hit, "Bei Mir Bistu Shein," Lacey and Mabel received a loud applause from the audience.

For the encore, however, Lacey sang "Embraceable" by herself. She got a standing ovation from several Italian tourists staying at the hotel. They even shouted, "Grandezza Stella" (the Great Star in English). From that day on, the nickname Stella stayed with Lacey wherever she performed.

It was still freezing in New York when the group returned from the Bahamas. Aaron had a party at his apartment to celebrate Lacey's success in the Bahamas.

"Our Stella is the best," Aaron said, toasting with a glass of wine in his hand.

"Let's drink to that," Szymon added.

On the way to Aaron's apartment, Szymon had picked up the *New York Times* at a kiosk. Aaron took a glimpse of the front page and read out loud, "In China, Mao Tse-tung is spreading communist doctrine. In Russia, Stalin rules with an iron fist." He looked at Szymon and continued, "Aha, Stalin. Are you familiar with the Polish-Bolshevik War of 1921*, Szymon?"

"Of course. I lost my father in this war," Szymon replied.

"I'm sorry to hear about your father. Let me tell you a little bit about my father's experience during this war. My father was not only wise, but a righteous and just Jew. He was also a Polish patriot. He volunteered and joined the Polish Army during the Polish-Bolshevik War because he didn't want Europe to fall into Communist hands. Someone had to stop them. My poor mother was in despair, crying every day when he left for this war," Aaron explained.

"Go on," Szymon insisted.

"My father explained to me how he met two American volunteer pilots, Cooper, Merian* and Fauntleroy, Cedric*. My father mentioned that they were both from well-to-do families on the East Coast. They were the best kind of people. They loved freedom. They were stationed in Paris with other pilots after World War I and decided to fly to Poland to support them in this war.

"From the air, their planes wiped out the famous Russian cavalry on the ground. Altogether, seventeen American pilots fought for Poland in this war, and five of them lost their lives," Aaron explained.

"I wonder why they decided to fight for Poland's independence?" Szymon asked, perplexed.

"My father asked them the same question," Aaron continued.

"And?" asked Szymon.

"They said they were only returning the favor from the time when Poles, including Kosciuszko and Pulaski, fought for American independence in the American Revolutionary War," Aaron continued.

"They were really great American patriots," Szymon added.

"Moreover, the pilots even knew about our Jewish Colonel Berek Joselewicz. Berek created the Jewish regiment in the Polish Army and fought together with Kosciuszko for American independence. My father was very impressed with them for knowing this piece of history," Aaron stopped.

"Now I know why we have a town named Poland in the state of New York and another in the state of Maine," Szymon added.

"Well, it was finally at the Battle of Warsaw* that the Red Army was defeated. White Poland overcame Red Russia," Aaron continued.

"It wasn't the first time that Poland saved Europe," Szymon said.

"Tell me about it," Aaron insisted.

"The first time Poland saved Europe was in 1683 during the Grand Vizier of the Ottoman Empire General Mustafa, Kara's* siege of Vienna. He promised to make stables for his horses out of Vatican City. He promised to destroy Judeo-Christian Europe. At that time, only Poland had a strong enough army to stop Mustafa. King Sobieski, Jan's Husaria*, known for battles throughout Europe, freed Vienna when it was besieged. After the great battle, Kara Mustafa committed suicide."

"Is that why the Turks have the utmost respect for Poles?" Aaron asked.

"It's possible," Szymon nodded.

"But back to the Battle of Warsaw, it was known as the Miracle on the Vistula."

"The Vistula River?"

"Yes, the Vistula that flows through Poland to the Baltic Sea."

"Do you know of any other such miracles?" Szymon asked.

"It's possible that throughout history, our rabbis' Jewish prophecies were part of these Polish miracles," Aaron added.

"It's a miracle that Poland has not perished!" Szymon said.

"Spain and Poland were the only countries to find honor in national declarations! God, honor, and homeland! What a vastly different worldview compared to a country like Switzerland that places so much value on neutrality. For Poles, there was no purgatory—there was only heaven or hell," Aaron stated.

"It's a chivalrous and proud nation, much like our United States of America. We say the same thing here: God, honor, country! These values are such a rarity in the world," Szymon added.

"It's amazing and maybe even a miracle that no invaders of Poland, whether Austrians, Germans, Mongols, Russians, Swedes, Tatars or Turks, have been able to steal our national treasure, the painting of the *Black Madonna** with a scar on her face. For centuries, diamonds, emeralds, rubies, sapphires, gold, silver, and other valuables worth millions of dollars have been placed at her altar on the hill of Jasna Gora's Monastery in the city of Czestochowa.

"The Polish kings and queens, aristocrats, and common believers who venerated her as the Queen of Poland were never touched by occupiers of Polish soil. Why? Because the occupiers were afraid of being cursed by the powerful image of the Black Madonna painted by Saint Luke, the Evangelist. In the year 1655, when Swedish King Charles X Gustav invaded Poland, monks and a handful of brave soldiers defended the monastery for forty days until the Swedes finally abandoned the siege. Fired up by what they thought to be a miracle, the Polish people rose up and successfully resisted their invaders." Aaron paused.

"Do you think the Black Madonna is our spiritual protector?" Szymon asked.

"There must be something to it because even Poland's rich Jewish aristocracy honored her with treasures and money. Why? Mark my words, one day, we will have a Polish pope who will visit the future country of Israel," Aaron finished his thoughts.

After observing Szymon for a few months, Aaron came to the conclusion that Szymon was unhappy. He had held a couple odd menial jobs and always seemed to be longing for something else. A few people saw him at New York's harbor checking on the transatlantic ships bound for Europe. Finally, Aaron decided to bring up the subject of the harbor visits to Szymon.

"It seems to me that you are constantly divided between your past and future, between two cities, the present one, New York, and the former, Bialystok, like Christ on the cross," Aaron muttered.

"Who?" Szymon asked.

"Like Jesus Christ."

"Why?"

"Did you like your hometown Bialystok?"

"I loved it. It was the fifth-most forested city in Poland," Szymon replied.

"So why didn't you stay there?"

"I wanted to see America."

Aaron forgot that he was holding Sienkiewicz, Henryk's* book, *Quo Vadis,* in his hands. He had just borrowed it from the library to reread it.

Szymon took a glimpse at the title.

"*Quo Vadis*? What does this mean in Latin?" he asked.

"It literally translates to 'Where are you marching?' Didn't you read Sienkiewicz's book about the early Christians during Nero's Rome?"

"I don't think so."

"Sienkiewicz won the Nobel Prize in literature for his trilogy novels that dramatized famous events in Poland's history."

"I read those," Szymon added.

"Speaking of *Quo Vadis*, I'll tell you what I remember from the first time I read it. In Rome, there was a church, Quo Vadis, dating back to the ninth century. It was situated on the Via Antica. According to legend, Saint Peter the Apostle took this road when he decided to leave Rome to avoid persecution. There he met Jesus and asked him, 'Domine, Quo Vadis?' which in English means 'My Lord, where are you going?' Jesus responded, 'Venio iterum crucifigi,' meaning 'I'm going to be crucified once more.' Saint Peter grasped the symbolic meaning of the answer and returned to the city to die a martyr's death."

"How tragic," a subdued Szymon replied.

Szymon was born to a Polish Catholic father and a Jewish mother. His mother had more influence on him throughout his life. Before he boarded a ship in Hamburg bound for New York, his mother insisted that he join a synagogue in the city. So he did. Since he was born in Bialystok, he joined the Bialystoker synagogue in New York, which was built in 1826 by Jewish immigrants from the city of Bialystok in Poland.

Since Christmas was quickly approaching, Lacey and Mabel decided to go shopping at Macy's to buy gifts for Aaron, Sam Rothstein, Szymon, and Mabel's aunt.

The next day, they took the subway to Harlem to visit Mabel's aunt. She was a pleasant woman working as a nurse in the hospital. Both girls, Lacey and Mabel, learned a great deal from her about the city's growing health problems. She thanked them for such an expensive gift and asked them to stay longer. The conversation was lively and went on for hours.

Since Aaron and Szymon immigrated from Poland, Lacey and Mabel became more and more curious about the country, its people, and its history. "And don't forget about famous Poles from American history like Tadeusz Kosciuszko after whom Americans named the town of Kosciusko in Mississippi," Aaron mentioned.

"I knew a few Polish people in Milwaukee," Lacey said, stretching her legs. "Szymon, please tell us more about Poland. After all, you were born there," Lacey insisted.

"Well, Polish history and Poland itself are very complex. Having the worst geographical place in the heart of Europe, Poland was always visited by her German neighbors to the west, Russian neighbors to the east, and even by Swedes in the north," Szymon began.

"I can only tell you about Poland from the Jewish perspective," Aaron answered.

"Should I give a quick lesson in Jewish-Polish history?" Szymon asked.

"Let me do it," Aaron insisted. "Jews came to Poland from both Byzantium* and Western Europe in the ninth century. In Poland, Jews had not been confined to ghettos like in England or other places in Europe, nor had they been obligated to pay taxes or perform physical labor," Aaron said.

"Go on," Szymon encouraged.

"In the fourteenth century, King Casimir the Great* ended a thirteen-year war against Teutonic Knights*. He was a great king! He encouraged Jewish industry and commerce. He founded the Jagiellonian University in Krakow. King Casimir had a Jewish lover named Esther. The king loved Esther so much that he would do anything for her. She requested a royal document that granted privileges and freedom to all Jews living in Poland."

"And did she get it?" Lacey asked.

"Absolutely. The king validated and legalized the presence of the Jewish minority in the country. He had two sons with Esther who later established one of the most famous noble families in Polish history." Aaron continued, "In the sixteenth century, when King Stefan Batory died, the wealthy Jewish banker, Saul Wahl Katzenellenbogen, was elected the next king of Poland.

"Although his last name was Katzenellenbogen, the Jews thought it was too long, so they simply called him Wahl, which came from the German word for election. There were shouts of joy when he was elected. Many Jews cheered, 'Long live King Saul!' King Saul passed many laws that improved conditions for Polish Jews. I could go on and on," continued Aaron.

"So continue. We're not bored," Lacey insisted.

"In the nineteenth century, the city of Lodz was considered by Jews to be the promised land. Lodz* was named 'Manchester of the South' for its textile industry. Owners of textile manufacturers built the most beautiful palaces in Europe. Most were built by Jewish industrialists like Karol Scheibler, Izrael Poznanski, Hinderman, Gorman, and others. Not to brag, but I visited three of these palaces before I came to New York," explained Aaron.

"Back in Poland, we kept our Jewish traditions. My mother asked me to pray four times on the Sabbath. During the Amidah prayer with two middle blessings, Kibutz and Galuyut, we asked God to bring us back from the Diaspora to Israel," Aaron concluded.

Back at the 200 Club, life continued as usual. Lacey, or Stella, and Mabel sang their usual repertoire every night.

One day, Sam Rothstein charged in, slamming the door and hollering, "Girls, I found two great songs for you to sing."

Both girls stood puzzled.

"'Night and Day'" and 'Begin the Beguine,'" Sam said.

Aaron wasn't around, so after distributing the music sheets with lyrics, Sam sat down and waited for Lacey and Mabel to take the stage. First, Lacey started to sing "Night and Day" with music and lyrics by Cole Porter.

Night and day, you are the one
Only you beneath the moon and under the sun
Whether near to me or far
It's no matter, darling, where you are
I think of you night and day, day and night.

When Lacey finished, Sam was impressed.

"Do you think you can handle the other song, Mabel?" he asked.

"I hope so," Mabel answered quietly.

Mabel started off so softly that Sam asked her to sing louder.

She started again with "Begin the Beguine" with music and lyrics by Cole Porter.

When they begin the beguine
It brings back the sound of music so tender
It brings back a night of tropical splendor
It brings back a memory ever green.

The year 1934 was coming to an end. New Yorkers were enjoying New Year's Eve across the whole city, but the 200 Club was the most popular place to be.

Lacey became a star again with her rendition of "Night and Day." The audience at the club shouted, "We want more Stella!"

And Mabel? Mabel sang "Begin the Beguine" beautifully and was cheered on by the crowds. The year ended on a happy note for both "stars" from the Midwest.

The Journey

The year was 1935. Everything was going smoothly at the 200 Club. Every night, Lacey and Mabel sang their repertoire. They were becoming more and more popular, especially among male audiences. Some men even left written messages for Lacey or Mabel asking for a date. However, both girls were not interested and always refused to meet any of the men. Aaron assumed that because of their Midwest family-oriented upbringing, they set their minds on their careers rather than getting involved with men.

Aaron suspected that both of them were still virgins.

Aaron wanted to give the girls a break, so he invited Lacey and Mabel to a classy restaurant. After both girls were seated at the table, Aaron excused himself to go to the men's room. On the way back, he noticed Sam Rothstein walking in with a lady companion. Aaron joined the girls at the table and observed Sam's friend for a moment. She looked extraordinary. In his mind, Aaron started to repeat a poem he had memorized about a woman he knew back in Warsaw: She was without fantasy, without delicate desires, glimmering with diamonds, smelling with freshness, and to be awakened with roses. With her elegance and beauty, he thought she looked like some rich man's trophy. Lacey and Mabel didn't notice anything unusual.

Sam Rothstein and his lady friend were seated three tables away from Aaron and the girls. While Aaron had great respect for his boss, he also knew that Sam frequently enjoyed the company of beautiful women and liked to gamble.

Aaron was very happy for Sam until, one day, everything changed. Sam was heading to the Bahamas to gamble. When he was at the railroad station leaving first for Miami, he noticed that he forgot his passport. He called Aaron to retrieve it for him. He explained that his neighbor had a spare key to his apartment, and the passport was in his desk drawer. Aaron couldn't say no to his boss. Although he knew that Sam liked gambling and women, he could never figure out in which order.

After finding the passport, Aaron took a quick glimpse at a note left laying open under the desk lamp. He started to read:

> My dearest!
>
> How are you? Are you all right? I'm still longing for you. I'm lonely without you. Thank you for your letters. I've memorized them. Please be careful when you're gambling.
>
> Love, Angela

While driving to the railroad station with the passport, he wondered whether Angela was the woman with Sam at the restaurant.

He wanted to find out who this Angela was. He asked everyone he knew, but no one was able to tell him anything. Everyone seemed afraid to even talk about it. Aaron couldn't understand why until, one day, he found a note under his door that read "Angela is Ignatzio Conti's wife. Tell Sam Rothstein to be extra careful."

Aaron had known about Ignatzio, the boss of the Camorra gang in Brooklyn. He was a very violent New York gangster who had killed many people. Ignatzio was not only known in New York circles, but he was infamous across the whole country.

When Aaron warned Sam about Ignatzio, Sam just shrugged his shoulders and walked away, not interested in what Aaron was saying. Aaron was very concerned about Sam but also about the future of the 200 Club.

Since it was summer, Lacey and Mabel only sang three nights a week. On Wednesday evening, they were on stage practicing one of their most popular hits, "Bei Mir Bistu Shein." Meanwhile, Sam asked Aaron to go upstairs to find a record he had promised Angela.

Suddenly, the outside doors of the club opened, and who barged in? Ignatzio Conti. He looked around and finally found Sam Rothstein. He ran toward the stage and approached Sam. His face was full of hate. He pulled out his gun, pointed it at Sam and screamed, "You son of a bitch, I don't care about the hundred thousand bucks you owe me, but you're not going to sleep with my wife, Angela, anymore." He shot Sam four times in the chest, instantly killing the famous owner of the 200 Club.

The girls stood on stage, helpless. As Ignatzio was running out of the club, he realized they were witnesses and shouted, "You're both dead. I'll find you. You won't escape."

Lacey and Mabel looked horrified and started crying after Ignatzio left. It was a ghastly scene.

Aaron had also heard the shots upstairs. He ran back down the stairs with Sam's record and noticed his body lying on the floor. He lamented, "Oh my god! Sam's dead! I never imagined that we'd have a murder on the stage of our great club."

Aaron heard Ignatzio's threatening words against his singers, and he knew he was not joking. "Goddamnit, the police won't prosecute Ignatzio for this crime. I hope, someday in the future, the government will set up programs that actually protect witnesses. We must save the girls, Szymon. Ignatzio is a vindictive and very vengeful ex-con," Aaron said.

"I'm scared," Mabel said.

"Better to be scared than dead," Szymon added.

After some thought, Aaron gathered his three best friends and drove them to Central Park so they could go for a walk where no one would hear them.

"Get out now!" Aaron ordered. "I want you to stay alive. Warsaw," he whispered. "Yes, we will send you to Warsaw! You will be safe there," Aaron said decisively.

Mabel knew that many New York elite who attended her shows had traveled to Europe, countries like France, Spain, England, Germany, to enjoy the museums, paintings, sculptures, and fine dining. But Poland?

"Listen," Aaron got angry. "People say that Warsaw is the Paris of the East," he added. "Would we be able to perform there?" Lacey asked.

"C'mon, there are many clubs and cabarets in Warsaw like Adria, Qui Pro Quo, Morskie Oko (Eye of the Sea), Buffo, Komedia, Melodia, and others. There are also many theaters, the most famous being the National Theater. My friend, Ben Rosen, even plays piano at the Panorama Theater. He was in his twenties when I left Poland for America. I still have his address on Prozna Street. I will contact him, and he can help you. Polish people like American music, especially jazz. I'm sure they will appreciate performers from America—both of you have so much talent, and most importantly, you will be safe there," Aaron finished.

"Are there any Black people in Warsaw?" Mabel asked.

"Not many, so I suspect Poles will be intrigued by you," Szymon added.

The girls' fear of Ignatzio was stronger than their fear of taking the voyage to Poland.

The next day, Aaron asked Szymon to find the itineraries of any transatlantic ships bound for Poland. Szymon recalled that the last time he went to the harbor was when he tried to board a ship to return to his city of Bialystok.

"The MS *Batory* is scheduled to leave on October 12, 1936, from New York through Copenhagen to Gdynia. There's also the MS *Pilsudski* going from New York through Halifax to Gdynia, leaving in a few days on August 25," Szymon announced.

"That's the one. We have no time to waste," said Aaron.

The girls already had their American passports from when they traveled to the Bahamas. Aaron visited the Polish Consulate to get visas for both Lacey and Mabel.

At the harbor, Aaron turned to the girls and gave a bon-voyage speech.

"Now you are ready to take the voyage of your lives. And where to? First to the Baltic harbor of Gdynia and then to Warsaw, known as the mecca of Jewish commerce, banking, and business, and often called the Yiddish capital of the world," Aaron finished with a smile.

Although the city of Gdansk, also known as the Free City of Danzig, was more familiar to the American public, Gdynia was newly established after the harbor was built there in 1920. Poles and other immigrants from neighboring countries like Belarus, Ukraine, Lithuania, Latvia, Estonia, and others could simply get on Polish Transatlantic in Gdynia and take a voyage to the United States or Canada.

Szymon couldn't help but give a quick history lesson about the ships in the harbor. While the MS *Batory* was named after a Polish king, the MS *Pilsudski* was named after the statesman and leader of the Legions who defeated Russia in the Polish-Bolshevik War.

The two American stars, Lacey and Mabel, were ready to board the MS *Pilsudski*. For a bon voyage gift, Aaron gave Lacey a pair of beautiful diamond earrings in the shape of the Star of David, which reminded him of his Jewish heritage.

"Wear them all the time, Lacey. They will bring you luck," Aaron said, kissing Lacey on both cheeks. He had tears in his eyes.

"Write to us and take care of Mabel," Szymon said, kissing both girls.

The girls boarded the MS *Pilsudski*, waving at Aaron and Szymon and knowing how much they had done for both of them.

Because of what happened at the club, these two singers from New York were on their way to Warsaw to begin their incredible journey.

They were assigned one cabin on the ship. As they slowly drifted toward the ocean, they went outside on the deck and enjoyed the New York skyline and the Statue of Liberty with the other passengers.

After learning about the girls' talents, members of the crew asked Lacey and Mabel to perform in the evening with a four-piece band that played during dinnertime.

The girls agreed and put on quite the show. Lacey sang "Night and Day," and Mabel sang "I Got Rhythm." The captain and crew loved their performance.

At breakfast, they were joined by one of the passengers who happened to be a member of the Polish Academy of Science.

"My name is Karol," he introduced himself. "I just returned from Palo Alto in California. I took part in a physics symposium at Stanford University. I was impressed by the knowledge presented by American scientists. And to top it all, they are so lucky to live in such a beautiful country."

Lacey and Mabel felt very proud to hear this from someone from a foreign country. When the gentleman asked them about the reason for their trip, they said they were just visiting a mutual friend in Warsaw.

It would take ten days to reach Gdynia. During sunny days, the girls came out to the deck, sat on the lounge chairs and absorbed the sun and prayed for no stormy days. But they did get seasick one day due to the stormy weather. When the ship was getting closer to the area where the famous *Titanic* had sunk, the ship slowed down so everybody could pay respect to the victims of this tragedy. Passengers watched the horizon in deep thought as they reflected on the sinking of this great ship.

During a conversation with their newly acquainted gentleman friend, the question of how the girls would get to Warsaw came up. They said they would get there by train.

"My chauffeur will pick me up. I'll gladly give you a ride to Warsaw. It's only about four hundred kilometers. I also forgot to tell you that I have a daughter named Anna. She is the same age as you. She will be happy to show you the city," Karol said.

In a few days, the two singers arrived at Gdynia's harbor. Mr. Karol, as Mabel called him, kept his word and gave them a ride to Warsaw in his limousine.

Lacey pulled out a piece of paper with the address Aaron gave her. "Take us to Prozna Street," Lacey said to the chauffeur.

"Voila, here we are," said Mr. Karol. "I hope you'll enjoy my beautiful city. It's not New York, of course, but it has its charm."

They were really happy that he gave them a ride to a city they didn't know yet.

Lacey knocked on the door of Ben Rosen's apartment. Ben opened the door to greet the girls. "Welcome to Warsaw. Did you have a nice trip? How is Aaron?" he said.

"Aaron sends his greetings. Mazel tov!" Lacey said, handing Ben the letter from Aaron.

"On Prozna Street, there are not too many rich people living here, like you have in New York. It is a very modest part of town, a mixture of people representing different professions, but many artists do live here. You can stay here until you'll find your own place to live. I'll help you look," Ben added.

Lacey already liked Ben and tried to win his attention. "Can we see the city?" Mabel asked.

"I also want you to get to know Warsaw's show business scene and its stars. There are many! Tomorrow, we'll visit three cabarets," Ben said proudly.

The next day, as Ben promised, he took the American girls to the Morskie Oko cabaret. It was an American show, Cole Porter's "Let's Misbehave." Lacey and Mabel enjoyed it very much, especially the jazz, shimmy, and foxtrots. Next, Ben took both girls to the Persian Eye cabaret to see Poland's biggest star Bodo, Eugeniusz's* performance as Jolson, Al's* from an American show.

"Did you like Bodo's stage musical?" Ben asked. "He's such a big cabaret and movie star. He is known as the Polish Chaney, Lon*. Actually, Bodo was born in Switzerland, but he came to Warsaw to sing, dance, and act in the movies. There are also other performers who came to Warsaw from various European cities to seek fame and fortune, just like you went to New York to fulfill your dreams to become singers. You'll meet some of them in time," Ben explained.

"Let's go to Melodia cabaret. There's always something nice to see there, especially the half-naked dancing girls," Ben murmured.

"So are all men like this? Always hoping to see half-naked dancers, Ben?" Mabel noticed.

"Today is a different kind of show. Ordonowna, Hanka* is performing. She is a singer with a very nice voice. I will try to introduce her to you. She is my close friend," Ben said.

Ordonka, as he called Hanka, started to sing one of her greatest hits in Polish, "Miłość Ci Wszystko Wybaczy" with music by Wars, Henryk* and lyrics by Tuwim, Julian*.

Ben translated the song's lyrics quickly so Lacey and Mabel could understand what the song was about:

Love will forgive you forever
Sorrow will change into laughter.
Love, which explains me so lovely:
Betrayal and lying and sin.
And if you'll curse in despairing,
That is so sadistic and fierce,
Love will forgive you forever.
For love, my dear darling, is me.

After the show, Ben invited Ordonka and the girls for a drink. Mabel ordered a mazagran, a drink with coffee, sugar, and rum. Lacey decided to get a polonezka with vodka and grenadine because it sounded so foreign and exotic. Hanka ordered a Manhattan in honor of her new American friends.

After Ben introduced Lacey and Mabel to Ordonka, she looked at them piercingly, saying: "Being singers from the United States, we'd be happy to use your American talents here. How about Komedia? Did you like it? But why Warsaw? Hollywood is the place to start a career. Our very own Apolonia Chalupiec, known as Negri, Pola*, went to Hollywood and has already starred in movies with Charlie Chaplin and Rudolf Valentino. Hollywood is definitely the place to be."

In his late thirties, Ben Rosen was a good piano player. He was scheduled to perform at the Panorama Theater in the evening. He asked the girls to tour the city but not by themselves. So the girls called Anna, the daughter of Mr. Karol from their transatlantic voyage, to show them around so they wouldn't get lost in a city they barely knew.

As Lacey, Mabel, and Anna walked the streets of Warsaw, what did they see? Ads and billboards with photos of the Polish movie star Bodo. They were everywhere!

"He must be a really big star here," Mabel said to Anna.

"Yes, he is. I adore him myself," Anna added.

Next, Anna pointed to billboards showing several female beauties, Bodo's movie partners. "Look here, it's a picture of Nora Ney, the Polish Greta Garbo. And look there, it's Ina Benita, the Polish Marlene Dietrich. Over there is Maria Bogda—what a beauty, just look at her fantastic long legs. I wish I had legs like these," Anna explained various details from the posters they were looking at.

"Incredible," Lacey murmured.

At this moment, Lacey recalled Aaron saying, "Warsaw is the Paris of the East," and she started to believe him.

Anna and the American girls ran into a street band with its leader playing an accordion and singing some song they didn't recognize. When the band's leader noticed that Lacey and Mabel were foreigners, he started to sing a very popular Warsaw song: "Szczescie Trzeba Rwac Jak Swieze Wisnie" with music by Wiktor Bialastocki and lyrics by Walery Jastrzebiec. Even though they didn't understand the lyrics, they found this song to be very beautiful.

Szczescie trzeba rwac jak swieze wisnie
Poki jeszcze czas, nim szczescie prysnie,
Chwycic szczescie, co masz sil.
Kochac, zyc, na jawie snic,
Ten sen, co sie w dziecinstwie snil.

When they returned home, Ben was already back from his concert. Lacey asked Ben to translate the lyrics of the song to English, and when he did, she started to hum:

Pick your fortune quick, like fresh, red cherries,
Choose the fortune quick like other berries.
Grab the fortune, hold it clean,
To love, to live in waking dream
This dream, which as a child was streamed.

"Well, I just heard that not only is Ordonka performing at Komedia but also some giant strongman. Let's go see this show," Ben said.

So they went. When they entered the theater, the show "Jew and Goy" was still going on. There were four dancers on the stage and very catchy music was playing, but the show was almost over.

"Goliath! Quickly! Goliath on the stage!" the stage manager hollered.

A giant man called Goliath entered the stage followed by six other men. As a part of the show, he lifted all six men and held them upright for a couple of minutes.

The audience gazed with awe. Lacey and Mabel were surprised by the variety of performances on the stage. There were actors, singers, and athletes all performing at the same show so everyone attending found something interesting.

But they came just to see Hanka Ordonowna, and she was performing next. She was singing Cole Porter's hit, "Just One More Chance," but the Polish version of it was "Nikt Tylko Ty."

Lacey started to hum "No One But You" in English.

"Remember, Mabel, when back in New York, Aaron asked us to sing 'No One but You'? That's why." and she pointed to the stage at Ordonka.

After Hanka finished her song, she approached Lacey and Mabel. She informed both girls of her meeting with the cabaret's owner and of his promise to give them a chance to perform at the Christmas and New Year's Eve shows. He said he would introduce them at the show as Hollywood stars.

Both girls could hardly believe what was happening; they promised Hanka Ordonowna to prepare the same repertoire they had done in New York.

Christmas was approaching in Warsaw, and Polish Christmas was filled with so many traditions. Decorating the Christmas tree, singing carols, delicious food, freshly baked bread, homemade cakes, gingerbread cookies, and babkas.

"Do you know of any Polish Christmas traditions?" Ben asked curiously.

Lacey and Mabel had no idea what he was talking about. They only knew of American customs and traditions.

Ben Rosen surprised them by preparing a white carp baked in the Jewish style with sweet and spicy sauce, full of raisins and almonds. All of his guests loved it. A white carp was considered a royal fish only in Poland and Japan.

After dinner, Ben quickly went to the other room and started to write something on a card he found on the table. Lacey followed him quietly and peeked over Ben's shoulder.

"I almost forgot. I'm writing a Hanukkah card to Aaron in New York," he told Lacey.

"You are such a good man, Ben, always remembering your friends," Lacey whispered.

"Now, everybody, let's go to Komedia. You can't be late for your first show," Ben Rosen ordered.

The two American girls from the Midwest and stars already in New York got to perform at Warsaw's exclusive cabaret Komedia for the first time. They sang "Bei Mir Bist Du Shein," their biggest hit, and Cole Porter's "Night and Day" and "Begin the Beguine."

Ben Rosen invited his friends in show business to see Lacey and Mabel perform, people from his circle like composer Henryk Wars, clarinetist Robert Felski (a Polish patriot deeply upset about Hitler's rise to power in Germany), singer Hannah Herman, who was planning to marry the son of a very important Warsaw rabbi (Ben promised Hannah to be at their wedding), harpist Rachel Bernstein, violinist Esther Bruskin, and others.

Also in the audience were Adam Czarny and Frederic von Ulrich. They seemed completely captivated by the two beautiful American performers. Adam Czarny preferred Mabel, and Frederic von Ulrich was fascinated by Lacey. He kept his eyes fixed on her. But who were Adam and Frederic? Well, they both were very interesting men.

Adam Czarny, a Pole, was the owner of a racing stable with Arabian horses near the Sluzewiec horse-racing track. Frederick von Ulrich was a German aristocrat who worked as an attaché at the German embassy in Warsaw.

When Lacey performed in Warsaw or on other important occasions, she wore the earrings Aaron gave her. However, every time she was on the stage, Ignatzio's face appeared in the back of her mind, reminding her of what happened in New York.

After the show, Ben introduced his friend, Henryk Wars, to Lacey and Mabel.

"This is the best composer in Warsaw. Henryk's real name is Warszawski, but he shortened it to Wars. He dreams about going to Hollywood and thinks his name will be easier to pronounce when he gets there. He wrote music for almost all of Bodo's movies. Maybe he'll write a song for you, Lacey," Ben suggested.

"It's possible. I will be happy to write a beautiful song for a beautiful American girl like Lacey," Henryk whispered.

Lacey, Frederick, and the Berlin Olympics

July 1936. Szymon brought a copy of the *New York Times* to Aaron's apartment and set it on the table. Aaron was just getting out of the shower.

"Aaron, can you believe all the major historical events that have happened in just the past year? Listen." He started to read aloud, "Alcoholics Anonymous was formed, the US Social Security Act was signed into law, the Gallup Poll was introduced, Amelia Earhart flew solo across the Pacific, the Volkswagen Beetle was launched in Germany, Persia is now known as Iran, the first Public Housing Project was launched in New York, nylon was introduced by Dupont, the Hoover Dam was completed on the Colorado River, Mussolini's Italy attacked Ethiopia—" He stopped. "Remember Mussolini, Aaron? Hitler's old friend?" Szymon noted.

*****

Ben Rosen finally found a spacious apartment near Lazienki Park for Lacey and Mabel. It was a beautiful summer day.

And who was a frequent visitor at Lacey's place? Of course, it was Frederick von Ulrich. He was obsessed with Lacey. He liked to take walks through this beautiful park just to be close to her.

This went on for months.

Lacey liked Frederick. Handsome, educated with delicate features, blond hair and blue eyes, he was a man of impeccable behavior and character. Lacey liked such qualities in a man. Although there was something she really liked about Ben Rosen.

Ben, Frederick, and Adam liked to stop by Lacey and Mabel's apartment just to have coffee and discuss Bodo's movies. Bodo's films were playing at almost every movie theater in Warsaw. Ben Rosen had Warsaw's newspaper, *Kurier Warszawski,* on his lap and started to read out loud Bodo's film titles: "*The Singer of Warsaw* at Majestic, *The Red Jester* at Apollo, *The American Scandal* at Colosseum, *The Body's Cult* at Capitol, *The Black Pearl* at Rialto."

"I'd like to see this movie," Mabel said.

"Which one?" Ben asked.

"*The Black Pearl,* of course," Mabel hinted.

Because of Mabel's request and the great reviews, all five went to see *The Black Pearl.* As soon as the movie ended, they all began discussing it. They loved Bodo's female costar who was not only beautiful but also a great actress.

"I love her brown skin," Mabel said.

Warsaw women idolized Bodo, who was very handsome with dark hair, a beautiful smile, immense charm, and boundless talent. Millions of female hearts fluttered enthusiastically at just the mention of his name.

The next day, Lacey and Mabel were at Ben's place and had read that Bodo was performing at the Persian Eye cabaret. He was supposed to sing his best-known hit, "I'm Such a Cold-Blooded Cad." But before Ben had a chance to put his jacket on, there was a knock at his door. When Ben opened it, he saw his best friend, Henryk Wars, standing in front of him.

Henryk seemed to be very excited about something. He brought with him a song he had written for Bodo's new movie. The song's title was "Sex Appeal." Lacey looked at the copy of the lyrics in English. Apparently, Henryk Wars was already planning for a future in Hollywood. Lacey started humming the song with music by Henryk Wars and lyrics by Emmanuel Schlechter.

We are strong, you're powerful—we're the weaker sex,
Yet we have something that you would like to have,

What's worth your strength—your fist and strong arm.
We women, though weaker, have one weapon against you.
Sex appeal, it's our women weapon,
Sex appeal, it's something that excites you,
Grace, style, chic
That's what we are winning you with a jiffy, ohhhh.

Although the song "Sex Appeal" was written for Bodo's movie, Ben felt that Henryk had written it with Lacey in mind.

Ben was right. Henryk Wars made sure that Lacey Starr would sing his song "Sex Appeal" in English at Komedia.

One day in July, Frederick visited Lacey. He had the German newspaper, the *Berliner Tageblatt*, with him. He flipped through some pages while drinking coffee.

"Would you like to know what's going on in the United States?" he asked.

"Please tell me," Lacey got curious.

"Well, let's see. In the state of New Jersey, the first American aircraft carrier, USS *Yorktown*, was built. It seems the United States wants to remain a strong country. Let's see some other news," he continued.

"The American writer, Margaret Mitchell, published her novel, *Gone with the Wind*. It's received great reviews," Frederick continued.

"It's probably an interesting story," Lacey said.

"I hope you are not from the state of Wisconsin," he said.

"Why?" Lacey asked.

"This July, temperatures in parts of Wisconsin reached 113 degrees Fahrenheit," Frederick announced.

"I hope there was at least low humidity," Lacey said.

"I have some distant relatives living in Superior, Wisconsin. Wisconsin is a state with a large German population. I bet you've heard of a place called Germantown," Frederick explained.

"I know where it is. It's not far from my birthplace, Mequon," Lacey nodded.

"Other members of my family moved across the Mississippi River to the adjoining state of Minnetonka," Frederick said.

"You mean Minnesota," Lacey corrected him.

"Exactly! I had no idea that you were from Wisconsin. Incredible," he commented.

"I love Wisconsin, but I moved to New York before I came here," she answered.

"In August this year, we'll have the Olympic Games in Berlin. The Fuhrer* will be very proud of the games. Lacey, why don't you join me on my trip to the Berlin Olympics? You'll see the Fuhrer, the Reichstag*, and other interesting places in Berlin," Frederick begged her.

"I would rather go to the Berlin National Gallery to see some paintings," Lacey said quietly.

"Fine, I'll take you to all the places you'd like to see," Frederick said, squeezing Lacey's hand.

"I know you have many friends in Berlin you'd probably like to see, but I'll only go if you promise not to leave me by myself at any time. I don't want to be lost in these large Olympic crowds," Lacey said.

"I promise," said Frederick, trying to kiss Lacey.

"You are not Frederick Chopin," Lacey gently rebuffed him with a smile.

However, she regretted her actions after she noticed that Frederick pulled a beautiful silver fox fur with matching hat out of a box he had brought to her apartment.

"Winters are cold in Poland, and I want you to be warm when this time comes," he said while wrapping her in this beautiful fur.

He noticed Lacey's Star of David diamond earrings but didn't say anything.

*****

The next day, with German precision, Frederick started preparing for their trip to Berlin. They left from the Warszawa Glowna railroad station in a very comfortable Pullman sleeping car.

Ten hours later, they arrived at Berlin's railroad station at Alexanderplatz, the most important transportation hub in Berlin.

Lacey was dazzled by all the shops, restaurants, and movie theaters. She stopped at one of the theaters just to check if any of Bodo's movies were playing, but at that time, there weren't any. However, when she saw that one of Marlene Dietrich's movies was playing, she asked Frederick if they could see it. After the movie, Frederick showed her the Brandenburg Gate, the Berlin Cathedral, and the Berlin Rotes Rathaus (the Red City Hall). "Alexanderplatz is named after the Russian Tsar, Alexander the First," Frederick explained.

Since Lacey was interested in seeing the Berlin National Gallery and all of its paintings, Frederick took her there.

Walking through the gallery, she was most interested in the German Romantics exhibition. She realized that she was in Nazi Germany and some of the so-called degenerate works were purged from the gallery, and nobody could see them anymore. She enjoyed the German Romantics exhibit nevertheless. Especially one painting she couldn't take her eyes off that portrayed two women: the first one, a young beauty, and sitting next to her was a tired old woman with wrinkles, a furrowed brow, and worn hands.

"Paintings are prayers to God," Lacey told Frederick.

"We can't make God forgive our sins," Frederick began waxing philosophical.

"Well, this is a crazy world, just look at Hitler," Lacey said.

Frederick kept quiet, unable to think about how to reply.

"You see, Lacey, it's not an idea that rules our world but rather the world is ruled by a whip," he replied.

With Frederick's Berlin connections, Lacey and Frederick were able to watch the Olympic games for a few days. Every day, the weather was perfect, and Lacey enjoyed the sun. One day, she overheard some tourist standing behind her saying, "Even the weather sympathizes with Nazis."

When the Olympics were over, Frederick's college friend, Hans, couldn't wait to meet Frederick's beautiful American guest. He invited Lacey and Frederick for dinner at his house.

Frederick hadn't seen his friend in years, but he was sure that he hadn't become a Nazi sympathizer per se. What Frederick didn't know was that Hans actually did adhere to the Nazi ideology. In his house, Lacey and Frederick saw many Nazi artifacts. Hans took them both to his sitting room in which he proudly showed a sculpture of an Aryan man—white, strong, looking up as if he was gazing toward the future.

"Look here," Hans pointed at the sculpture. "Have you ever seen such athletes in the Olympics?" he bragged.

"Well, we just witnessed American athlete, Jesse Owens, win four gold medals at your Berlin Olympics. By the way, your Fuhrer wouldn't even congratulate Jesse for his great accomplishments," Lacey said angrily.

Frederick didn't say a word and kept quiet.

Hans' face got red with anger; he was ready to ask Lacey and Frederick to leave his house. They decided to leave as quickly as possible without ever mentioning the incident again.

Before this incident, Lacey was planning to get romantically involved with Frederick, especially after seeing the German Romantic exhibit, but she had become cold and uninterested in sex after what took place at Hans' house. However, she could see herself falling for Frederick.

Thus, the trip to Berlin, although remarkable, came to an end on such a sour note. Lacey Starr and Frederick von Ulrich had finally returned to Warsaw.

Lacey realized that while she was in Berlin, she had longed for Ben Rosen and Komedia cabaret; she was excited to be back in Warsaw and felt ready to sing Henryk Wars' sexy titled song "Sex Appeal."

Adam Czarny's Desire for Mabel and the Wedding of Hannah Herman and Jakub Lerski

February 1937. After what happened in Berlin, Lacey started to like Warsaw more and more. She recalled Aaron saying, "Warsaw is the Paris of the East," back when she was in New York. Almost everyone from Ben Rosen's entourage came to Komedia to hear Lacey sing "Sex Appeal." Regulars in Ben's company were usually Robert Felski, a clarinetist, and Kazimierz Krukowski, a comedian who always gave stinging satire on Polish politics. Both of them were performing at Komedia that night. There was also Marian Hemar, a poet, and Jerzy Petersburski, a composer. Finally, there was Ben's friend, Ludwik Hirszfeld, a microbiologist who Ben always called "the unknown Polish-Jewish genius."

When Lacey finished singing, Mr. Hirszfeld asked for her autograph. After Lacey's performance, the Swedish diva, Elna Gisfeldt, sang the operetta, "The Parisian."

"I saw Elna in 'Merry Widow,' 'Countess Maritza,' and 'The Queen of Tango.' A spectacular voice," Ben added.

The great Bodo was even in the audience. When he learned that Lacey was an American from New York, he joined Ben at his table after the show.

Bodo turned to Lacey, looking at her with dreamy eyes, and said, "I love the King of Swing, Benny Goodman, and other big bands of America."

Lacey respected Bodo's opinions because Ben Rosen told her that Bodo had even worked in the American movie industry with

Columbia Pictures and Universal Studios. She could hardly believe that she was sitting next to such a big star. Lacey learned that Bodo was planning his next tour to Palestine, Tel Aviv, and Haifa. Lacey asked if he spoke Hebrew, but he said that he would sing in Polish, and he predicted the audience would still love it.

Adam Czarny was fluent in English. Every year, he traveled to Ireland and worked at the Irish Champion Stakes and the Irish Derby. He was a faithful fan of Mabel at Komedia.

One night, after her performance, he asked her out for a date.

The next day, he picked her up at her Lazienki Park apartment in a horse-drawn carriage. Mabel came out wrapped around in a fur coat to keep herself warm.

"I'm glad Lacey lent me her fur coat and hat," she said shivering.

Adam took her to his stables at Sluzewiec, a subdivision of Warsaw. "I hope you'll like my horses," he said.

Adam pulled a black stallion out of one of the stables. Mabel got scared. The black stallion licked Adam's face.

"His name is Champ," Adam explained.

"Do you want to hear how much I know about horses?" Mabel asked.

"Sure. Go ahead," Adam was curious.

"When I used to live in Chicago, my father took me once to South Dakota, and we saw a herd of beautiful mustangs running freely on the prairie," Mabel said.

"Mustangs are special horses. All horses are a gift from heaven," Adam said. "Let me tell you. After God created horses, he sent them to the four corners of the globe to serve men. They can be hitched to a carriage or carry two newlyweds on their backs. A horse, like a woman, is a puzzle!" Adam hinted.

"It's interesting," Mabel commented.

"Too bad that only fairy tales have happy endings," Adam said.

Mabel wrapped herself closely in Lacey's fox fur.

"Some people would say that a horse is a stupid animal, but they don't really know them," Adam explained. Adam suddenly grabbed Champ's front right leg. "I saved this horse. He had a torn ligament.

I spent many sleepless nights caring for him. He never forgot that I did this for him. He loves me," Adam said.

"Do you think a horse can be as loyal as a dog?" Mabel asked.

"Noble as a horse is a true saying. Mabel, just try to hit me, and we'll see what happens?"

Mabel raised her arm toward Adam. Champ stood up on his back legs and tried to hit Mabel who backed out scared.

"Is there a better friend? Is there a girl who could love me like that?" Adam asked.

"Find out for yourself. You know nothing about Black girls," Mabel responded.

"It's ironic that my last name is Czarny, which in English means black," Adam said.

"Well, how convenient," Mabel responded.

"I would like to know you better. I can't stop thinking about your beautiful caramel-colored skin," Adam said.

"Really? Your lying eyes have a canny, childish look," Mabel responded.

"It's a perfect day to go on a sleigh ride. It's called *kulig* in Polish. Have you ever gone on one?" Adam asked.

"Not yet, but I always wanted to visit Aspen, Colorado, and try it," Mabel answered.

Adam prepared a sleigh pulled by two horses. "These horses are very gentle," Adam explained.

Mabel wrapped herself even closer in Lacey's fur and got into the sleigh. At first, they moved slowly, but then Adam made the horses gallop. Soon, Adam and Mabel were riding among a beautiful wall of pine trees. Mabel's hat flew away. Adam stopped the sleigh and gave the reins to Mabel.

"Hold them tight, don't be scared," Adam ordered.

Adam got out of the sleigh and ran back to pick up Mabel's hat. At that moment, a big bison came out of the forest and walked toward the sleigh. The bison was curious and touched Mabel with its snout.

"Adam! Help! Buffalo! Help! Come quickly, please!" Mabel screamed.

Adam grabbed the reins from Mabel and gave her the hat. "Don't be scared. It's only a European bison. Buffalos only roam the American West," Adam explained.

"I've only seen them in movies," Mabel said.

"According to American Indians, the buffalo is a sacred animal," Adam added.

"Are there also wolves out here?" Mabel asked.

"Probably, but don't be scared. I'm here with you," Adam replied.

The sleigh ride continued for at least an hour. Mabel admired the tall snow-covered pine trees. It was time to go back to Warsaw.

Adam Czarny was absolutely captivated by Mabel. The next day, he sent a taxi to pick up Mabel and bring her to his place. He showed her around his house. They sat down to enjoy some wine, and finally, he led her to his bedroom. She followed him knowing what might happen next. He slowly undressed her and asked if he could touch her beautiful skin. Adam caressed her body, kissed her neck, and murmured, "Passion is universal." His hands were all over her, and she liked his gentleness. He didn't rush to lovemaking, instead waiting for her to find pleasure in what he was doing.

"You are taking it a bit too far," she said quietly but didn't oppose it.

"I want you to be mine, my American beauty," Adam said, holding her tight.

He wanted to kiss every inch of her. He wanted to run his fingers through Mabel's hair. Her beautiful thick black hair made Adam go crazy. However, he was still torn between wanting Mabel's love or just giving in to playful pleasure.

Mabel was excited, thrilled, electrified. Adrenaline was pumping through her body. She gave into the sensation of him touching her. Adam stroked her full breasts; Mabel's moans grew louder.

He caressed her body with his tongue. They were both wrapped in a vortex of passion and ecstasy.

"Have you ever been with a woman like me?" Mabel asked.

"No, never. I love your silky caramel-colored skin," Adam whispered.

"I wish I had a lighter skin complexion, even white," Mabel said.

"Mabel, remember the movie *The Black Pearl*? What are you talking about? You are perfect the way you are," Adam protested.

Their lovemaking lasted until May.

Adam loved spoiling Mabel by bringing over her favorite French wine. She sipped her wine, gently touching the edge of her glass. He looked at her full lips and said, "I like your lips, I like your skin, I like all of you. I'm completely consumed by you."

"I'm consumed by your horses," Mabel jokingly answered.

"Now do you believe me that horses were made in heaven?" Adam asked.

"I'm starting to believe you," Mabel murmured.

"I saw many beautiful horses in Ireland," Adam responded.

"Lacey and I were discussing a possible visit to Ireland. Maybe one day," Mabel replied.

It was May 8, 1937. After he finished reading *Kurier Warszawski*, Frederick von Ulrich ran through the park toward Lacey's apartment. He was out of breath when he finally got there. And what did he find when he arrived? Lacey, Mabel, and Ben Rosen discussing the girls' repertoire at Komedia.

"Have you heard about what happened yesterday in New Jersey?"

"No," Lacey responded.

"The Hindenburg airship disaster at Lakehurst Naval Air Station in Lakehurst Borough," Frederick said quickly.

"Where was it coming from?" Mabel asked curiously.

"Frankfurt in Germany, but it caught fire and quickly became engulfed in flames. I feel sorry for the people lost in the fire," Frederick explained.

However, being German, Frederick wouldn't elaborate on the reason for the disaster. He realized that the Hindenburg was owned by Hitler's Nazi Germany, and the potential culprits were likely enemies of the Third Reich, like the thousands of socialists worldwide or maybe even some crew members on the Hindenburg.

June was quickly approaching, the month of Hannah's wedding.

Robert Felski, the clarinetist at the Komedia cabaret, was a Gentile, but he was dating Esther Bruskin who was Jewish. Esther performed every night at Komedia and afterward enjoyed listening to Robert play his clarinet. And he played it with all his soul.

Esther's mother liked Robert a lot, but because of religious traditions, she preferred if Esther dated a Jewish boy. However, Esther loved the great clarinetist from Komedia. Esther recalled Bodo's comments about Benny Goodman—"I love the King of Swing of America"—so she came up with her own saying, "I love the King of Swing at Komedia" every time she talked about Robert Felski.

One day before Hannah's wedding, Robert visited Esther. A large seven-branched menorah was staring at him from the corner table. Esther noticed his reaction. He walked by it slowly and carefully, afraid to accidentally touch it.

"In Hebrew, it simply means lamp," Esther explained.

"I hope you didn't forget about Hannah's wedding," Robert asked.

"Do you think I would forget about such an important date? Never in a million years," Esther replied.

On a warm June day at the Great Synagogue of Warsaw, Hannah Herman, a singer at Komedia, married Jakub Lerski, the son of a very important and influential Warsaw rabbi, Zvi Lerski. The traditional Jewish wedding ceremony started with "ketubah," a marriage contract signed by two witnesses. Then they stood under a "chuppah" canopy, where the groom gave the bride a ring. Finally, they stomped on a glass inside a cloth bag to shatter it. The newlyweds looked beautiful and very happy.

After the ceremonies at the synagogue, the celebration moved to the Bristol Hotel, Warsaw's most elegant hotel. All of Warsaw's Jewish and Gentile elite were there. It seemed like the whole city took part in the celebration. Even Stefan Starzynski, the mayor of Warsaw, and his wife were in attendance.

Rabbi Zvi Lerski was not only well-known in Warsaw, but he was quite respected in many of Poland's neighboring countries. There were even foreign guests at the reception.

Frederick stepped on Lacey's foot while entering the reception room.

"Wow! I'd like to murder you," Lacey shouted.

All of the guests diverted their attention to Lacey.

"Leave murders to Shakespeare," Frederick replied laughing.

They approached Ben Rosen, who was contemplating the seating arrangements for his group. "Who is sitting by whom?" he elaborated.

Rachel Bernstein sat by Henryk Wars. Mabel Brown snuggled up to Adam Czarny, of course. Esther Bruskin nestled close to Robert Felski, and Lacey Starr held her face against Frederick von Ulrich's chest.

Mabel noticed Bodo walking in with three ladies.

"Look, look, Bodo is here!" she exclaimed.

Bodo was getting everybody's attention.

"As usual, Bodo is surrounded by women," Adam commented.

"Well, he is a big movie star," Lacey responded.

When Ben Rosen's group finally settled down, Ben ordered a couple bottles of French wine, some champagne, and a bottle of Sherry Cordial.

The reception started, and the orchestra began to play an Argentinian tango. Robert stood up first and asked Esther for a dance. At first, all eyes turned to the dancing couple. Esther and Robert started dancing to the sounds of "La Cumparsita."

They were a beautiful couple. They moved to the rhythm of music, following a set sequence of steps. Their cheeks were pressed together as they danced.

"You are a good dancer, Robert, but you are a better clarinetist, you know," Esther whispered in his ear.

"Is this why we're together? Remember, I'm just a goy," Robert replied.

"I like goy men, I like Jewish men, I like tall men like you," she whispered.

"Then do you like gentle Gentiles?" he asked.

"As long as they are not Nazis," Esther replied.

"Can you believe it, Esther? This Austrian clown became the chancellor of Germany," Robert added.

"He is the devil incarnate," Ester replied.

"Every man is different. Adam likes Black girls like Mabel, but I like Jewish girls because there is something biblical in their nature," Robert said.

"Stop talking, just dance," Esther replied, squeezing him closer to her while dancing.

Adam became a little jealous of Esther and Robert's embrace and asked Mabel to dance. Frederick felt the same and bowed in front of Lacey, showing off his German class and escorted her to the dancing floor.

Everyone in Ben Rosen's group was now dancing.

When the music stopped, and all of the couples had returned to Ben's table, he raised a glass of champagne and made a toast to the newlyweds.

The wedding reception lasted until the early morning hours. As Rosen's party was getting ready to leave, Rabbi Zvi showed up at Ben's table, eager to meet two American stars from Komedia he had heard so much about.

Noticing a famous rabbi approaching the table, a tipsy Frederick stopped him and asked a question that no one could answer.

"Excuse me, Rabbi Zvi. Do you think the same God who created the sun so we could exist also anticipated it would radiate us with its warmth?" Frederick asked.

"Well, my son. As you know, there are no two suns for sure, but at least God made certain that human beings like you and me were given a pair of hands and feet," replied a smiling Rabbi Zvi.

Ben's guests applauded Rabbi Zvi and then left the wedding celebration tipsy but happy.

After the wedding, Lacey and Mabel gossiped about who danced with whom, who was tipsy, and who drank the most alcohol. They even remembered Rabbi Zvi's answer to Frederick's question.

The newlyweds departed for their honeymoon to the beautiful island of Ibiza, off the Spanish coast.

Up to this point, Lacey and Mabel were enjoying their stay in Warsaw.

Walking the streets of Warsaw in late July, Lacey, Mabel, Adam, and Ben ran into a crowd of rowdy protesters holding all kinds of posters. Lacey and Mabel didn't know what to expect and seemed a little scared. They looked at Ben who quickly explained the situation.

"This group is a Jewish organization, Das Bund, that wants Palestine divided into two separate states—Arab and Jewish. They want to leave a diaspora country like Poland and immigrate to Palestine. For one thousand years, we Jews stayed in Poland, but this group wants to have their own country, Israel. They are walking to the Market Hall to hear words of encouragement from Ben-Gurion, David* who was visiting from Palestine to share his experiences," explained Ben.

Mabel and Adam didn't pay attention to Ben's explanation of this situation; they were in love, and only this counted.

"He is my heart and my soul," Mabel told Lacey whenever she talked about Adam.

"I wish I could say the same about Frederick," Lacey replied.

All the while, no one knew that Ben was secretly in love with Lacey.

Knowing that Mabel went to see Adam, Ben bought a bouquet of red roses and went to visit Lacey at her place. Before he reached her apartment, he noticed Frederick's car parked in front. At first, he wanted to throw the roses in the garbage, but instead, he went to Lazienki Park and stood there for a long time, holding the roses and feeling disappointed and hurt.

However, he was a strong man, so he felt that another opportunity might come up some day to reveal his true feelings.

When Hannah returned from her honeymoon, she invited Lacey and Mabel to her recital at Komedia. She sang a beautiful song titled "Rebecca" about a Jewish girl. She told Lacey that she could perform this song instead of her at Komedia if she wanted.

It took Lacey a week to learn it, but when she finally sang it from the depths of her soul, it brought tears to the eyes of everyone in the audience. Since Lacey and Mabel began performing, there was a full house of guests every night at Komedia. The owner was elated, and Ben Rosen was very proud of the girls.

The lyrics to "Rebecca" were as follows, with music by Zygmunt Bialostocki and lyrics by Andrzej Wlast:

Oh my dear one,
Oh my missed one,
You don't know about it,
That there's someone in a little town,
Who is crying for you,
That poor Rebecca.
Is waiting in reverie,
Until you alone come to her,
And take her as your wife,
Far away, to the gates of the palace.
That rush, that glow, that miracle,
I can't imagine, my god!
There's crowd at the market square,
And I'm wearing a white wedding dress.
Oh my dreamt one,
Oh my missed one.

It was the Christmas season of 1937. It was time to start celebrating the holidays. Adam brought a Christmas tree to Lacey and Mabel's place that he cut himself in the forest. Robert and Esther brought over a few bottles of Italian wine; Frederick, of course, didn't want to come empty-handed, so he showed up with a bottle of German white wine. To keep it as an international affair, Ben Rosen brought a couple of his favorite French wines.

Ben also picked up *Kurier Warszawski* at the kiosk nearby to surprise Mabel and Lacey with news from the United States. Both girls, Lacey and Mabel, were listening with great attention to what he had to say.

"Well, in September, Austrian movie star Hedy Lamarr arrived in New York to divorce her husband, who made arms agreement with the Nazis," Ben read.

"Seems like no one likes the Nazis," Frederick added.

"Go on," Lacey urged Ben.

"In October, Ernest Hemingway's novel *To Have and Have Not* was published in New York," Ben continued. "I bet Aaron read it already," Ben added.

"In December, Walt Disney's *Snow White and the Seven Dwarfs* opened in Los Angeles," Ben read.

"Most likely with great success," Mabel added.

After that, Ben Rosen invited Lacey, Mabel, and his other friends to his place for a New Year's Eve party. They took all the wine they previously had at Lacey and Mabel's apartment and started a celebration to say goodbye to the year 1937.

Ludwik Hirszfeld, the Unknown Jewish Genius, and Warsaw's Three Black Gentlemen

In 1938, Warsaw was a bustling cosmopolitan city with a population of over one million.

May 12 was Lacey's birthday. Frederick knocked at the door of Lacey and Mabel's apartment, and when Lacey opened it, he kissed her on the cheek and went in to celebrate her birthday. Ben Rosen and Lacey's friends were already there. Frederick was keeping a secret from Lacey. He had bought her an expensive diamond necklace when they both visited the Berlin Olympics. With everyone in the room watching, he took the necklace out of its case and placed it around Lacey's long neck. With the diamond earrings she got from Aaron in New York and this necklace, she looked spectacular.

Of course, when Adam Czarny, Mabel's lover, saw Frederick give Lacey such a beautiful and expensive gift, he didn't want to feel cheap, so he stayed quiet. He was too proud.

The next day, he went to the most famous jeweler in Warsaw, Michal Mankielewicz, known as Mankiel for short. Mankiel was where the richest Varsovians shopped and where Russian oligarchs bought beautiful jewelry for their Anna Kareninas. Mankiel was a great patron of the arts, and he was known for giving female models and artists the most beautiful and priceless pieces of jewelry as gifts, especially to performers from Komedia.

Adam went to Mankiel's shop to buy Mabel a diamond necklace and matching bracelet. On a lovely spring day in May, Ben Rosen was surprised by a visit from his friend, Ludwik Hirszfeld, whom he had nicknamed the unknown Jewish genius. And the reason for his visit? Hirszfeld was so impressed with Lacey and Mabel's talent when he attended their performance at Komedia that he had to meet them. The night he attended their show, Lacey sang "Sex Appeal," and Mabel performed Cole Porter's "Night and Day."

Ben took Hirszfeld to visit Lacey and Mabel at Lazienki Park. After introducing him to the girls, they all sat on the couch and started chatting.

"I came to tell you that I have a daughter named Marysia. She is almost sixteen. I'd like you to meet her. She will be happy to speak a few words of English with you," he began.

"We would be happy to meet your daughter," Lacey said and Mabel agreed.

"Years ago, I was sought by four American universities including Stanford in California, but I declined," he said.

"Why?" Lacey asked with curiosity.

"I couldn't leave my wife, Hanna, my daughter, Marysia, and my beloved Warsaw, especially when I was named full professor at the University of Warsaw in 1931," Hirszfeld answered.

"Too bad," Mabel added.

"I know. I would have seen so much had I gone to America," Hirszfeld replied.

When Hirszfeld left, Ben Rosen told them a little more about Hirszfeld's story.

"Ben, please tell us, why did you call Professor Hirszfeld the unknown Jewish genius?" asked Lacey.

"Simply because 99 percent of people do not know who Hirszfeld is and all he has accomplished," Ben replied.

"And should they?" Mabel asked.

"Absolutely. He should be known and admired across the world. He codiscovered the A, B, and O blood types, which is so important for humankind," Ben said.

"Please tell us more," Lacey urged Ben. "Then sit comfortably and listen," Ben started.

"Hirszfeld is a microbiologist and serologist. He has a fantastic mind. He conducted his first experiments on rabbits. He discovered that if blood of rabbit number one was given to rabbit number two, it would kill rabbit number two. There was a conflict between blood types.

"Ludwik was born at the end of the nineteenth century to a Jewish family in the city of Lodz in Poland. Lodz was known by Polish Jews as 'the promised land.' He was the cousin of Aleksander Rajchman, a Polish mathematician, and Ludwik Rajchman, a Polish bacteriologist. His father was a banker.

"He started his medical studies in Berlin in 1904. Later he moved to Heidelberg, where he became an assistant to Emil van Dungern's Cancer Clinic. Hirszfeld and van Dungern both codiscovered the A, B, and O blood types. Their research demonstrated that blood groups A and B did not occur in offspring unless they were present in at least one of the parents, fulfilling the Mendelian principles of inheritance. They also showed that A and B were dominant traits, while O was recessive.

"Next, Hirszfeld moved to the University of Zurich's Hygiene Institute in Switzerland. In 1912, he married Hanna Kasman, also a physician. He always called her Hanka for short. She became an assistant at the Zurich Children's Clinic. In 1914, Hirszfeld was made an academic lecturer because of his work on anaphylaxis and anaphylatoxin and their relationship to coagulation.

"When World War I broke out, Hirszfeld moved to Serbia, which was being ravaged by dual epidemics of typhus and dysentery. He remained with the Serbian army until the end of the war. Also, during this time at a hospital for contagious diseases in Thessaloniki, Greece, he discovered the bacillus salmonella paratyphi c, which, today, is named salmonella hirszfeldi, after him. He saved thousands of Serbians and is considered a national hero of Serbia.

"As a doctor in the Allied Army of the Orient, together with his wife, he tested over 8,000 people from sixteen different ethnic groups and discovered that the frequency of blood groups differs depending on ethnic background. For instance, group A was common in people from Western Europe, like the English, Irish, Dutch, and French, while group B was more common among Asians, Africans, Russians, and Jews. Hirszfeld's report was published in 1919 in a respectable medical journal, *The Lancet*, and was the first paper to show that blood group frequencies differ between populations." Ben finished his story.

"Incredible," said Mabel.

"Now you know why I call Hirszfeld a genius," Ben Rosen added. "I have another story for you if you want me to continue," Ben asked.

"Go on," said Lacey.

"It was 1938, and there were three Black gentlemen residing in Warsaw. The first one was an American, very well-known by many Varsovians, practically a celebrity. He was tall, elegant, classy, and usually wearing a white suit with a white hat. Varsovians gossiped but actually didn't know much about him. Some said he was a banker, but no one knew for sure. Many said he came from America from the town of Kosciusko or Pulaski in the state of Mississippi. Others rumored that he came to Warsaw because he wanted to see the country, which both military leaders Kosciuszko and Pulaski came from to fight alongside the Americans in the Revolutionary War. No one knew him very well, so many Varsovians just called him Mr. Mississippi.

"The second Black gentleman was a saxophonist who played at Komedia cabaret. His name was Julien Scott. And how did he find himself in Warsaw? Initially he moved from the French colony of Senegal to Paris. He was a wonderful saxophonist, so he was immediately hired by the Parisian Moulin Rouge cabaret. The owner of Komedia was traveling through Europe in search of some talented performers to join his cabaret. He found Scott at Moulin Rouge and asked if he would be interested in coming to Warsaw and playing at Komedia. Some people said that he snatched Scott outright for his cabaret, and the rest was history as they say.

"The third Black man was August Agboola Browne. He was a jazz percussionist at Komedia. He was in his forties, born in Lagos, Nigeria, which was part of the British Empire at the time. He traveled to England on a British merchant ship. From there, he joined a theater troupe touring Europe and settled in Poland after a stint in Germany. Why Poland? It's possible that he liked Polish women because he married Zofia Pykwona, and they had two sons, Ryszard and Aleksander," Ben finished his story.

The year 1938 was the year Nazi Germany elevated its propaganda campaign.

It was the end of June. As usual, Frederick brought the *Kurier Warszawski* to Lacey and Mabel's place. He read the front page and passed the sports highlights over to Ben. Frederick looked disappointed.

"Can you believe American heavyweight boxer Joe Louis knocked out my beloved German boxer Max Schmeling at Yankee Stadium in New York? Incredible," Frederick said, almost crying.

Lacey felt sorry for Frederick, but inside, she felt a burning pride and happiness for an American success story. She understood Frederick von Ulrich's sadness. After all, he was a German patriot. Mabel was elated, ready to make a toast with her glass of wine to a great victory by an even greater American.

Ben noticed more important news on the front page of the paper. In May, there was an Anschluss (annexation) of Austria and an overtaking of Czechoslovakia's Sudetenland by Nazi Germany.

Whenever Lacey, Mabel, and Ben listened to Hitler's speeches on the radio, they felt his threatening tone, but Frederick reassured them that there was nothing to worry about. "It's just empty Nazi propaganda. People in Germany ignore it," he was always saying.

Meanwhile, Adam Czarny was still in love with Mabel. He always asked her to stay at his place, and she never refused. She enjoyed visiting his beautiful horses at the track. Even more, she enjoyed making love to Adam.

During the warm summer months of July, August, and September, Adam, Mabel, and their friends, Esther, Robert, Lacey, Frederick, and Ben, went to suntan by the Vistula River. They played volleyball and sometimes jumped in the river to cool off. They all enjoyed the beautiful summer days.

One day in October, when Frederick's car was in the shop, Ben Rosen picked him up so they could go see Eugeniusz Bodo's new movie at the Palace theater. On the way to the theater, Ben stopped to grab the latest edition of *Kurier Warszawski* at the nearest kiosk.

Frederick immediately started reading the newspaper. "The Nazi German government expels 12,000 Polish Jews from Germany back to Poland," he read.

"Incredible," Ben commented.

"What do they want from the Jews?" Frederick protested angrily.

"Ignore it. It is all propaganda," Ben replied.

"In November 1938 when Kristallnacht (Crystal Night) or the 'Night of Broken Glass' happened and Jewish businesses and synagogues were destroyed throughout Germany, it wasn't just propaganda," Frederick added.

"I don't understand. The Jews chose to live in Germany and had always been faithful to this country. Germany is a remarkably wise nation. It has many famous philosophers, scientists, and artists. I just can't comprehend how this could happen in the heart of Europe," Ben stated.

It was December 1938. Frederick stopped over at Lacey's apartment with the latest *Kurier Warszawski* and couldn't believe what he was reading.

"Can you believe it? Adolf Hitler was named *Time* magazine's 'Man of the Year.' I'm telling you, Europe is getting more and more dangerous," Frederick said.

Frederick's comments scared Lacey. She was getting really concerned about the whole situation in Europe. After all, Aaron assured her, back in New York, that Warsaw would be the safest place for her and Mabel. So far, there wasn't any news from New York about Ignatzio Conti.

Lately, Ben Rosen had been spending a significant amount of time at his piano in preparation for an important upcoming concert with other Polish artists at the Ateneum Theater.

"I'll be playing Chopin's 'Concerto in E Minor, Opus 11.' It seems the concert will have a patriotic tone due to all the menacing happenings around us," Ben stated.

"Can Mabel and I take part in it?" Lacey asked politely.

"It would be fantastic if you could showcase your American talents, but this concert is a patriotic event, and only Polish artists like the great Bodo or the Polish tenor, Kiepura, Jan*, will be performing. You'll definitely enjoy Kiepura's arias," Ben explained.

The day of the concert had finally arrived. Familiar faces could be seen all over the Ateneum Theater's lobby, including those of Esther, Robert, Hannah, and Jakub. The lobby was also filled with elegant women dressed in fur and wearing stunning jewelry, ordering champagne before the show. Even Warsaw's president showed up with his wife. Mabel wanted to fit in with the crowd, so she wore the diamond necklace and bracelet she received from Adam. Lacey also showed up with Frederick, wearing the diamond necklace he gifted her as well as the earrings she got from Aaron back in New York.

The curtain went up, and the concert began.

Ben Rosen sat at the piano and started playing Chopin's "Concerto" like he had promised. He was fantastic, putting his whole heart and soul into the music. The audience was not disappointed, and he received a standing ovation when he finished.

The audience didn't have to wait too long for the next performer. When Bodo walked on stage, he mimicked Charlie Chaplin's way of walking. There was an uproar of laughter. Bodo announced that he would sing "Titine" from Charlie Chaplin's movie, *Modern Times*. The music was by Leo Daniderff and lyrics by Louis Mauba and Marcel Bertel. However, the Polish lyrics were written by Andrzej Wlast, Marian Hemar, and Julian Tuwim.

Bodo started singing:

This poise, this look, this mustache,
This gaze, this curl, this laughter,
And grace, and fear, and grimace,
And laugh? Yes, yes, it's me.
Ach ladies, poor and wealthy,
This laugh, this laugh is so healthy,
Titine, aah Titine,
This simple song of mine.
La, la, la, la, la, la, la.

Bodo fingered his Chaplinesque mustache and continued singing.

But life's a stage, so I found a clone,
And lately on my humble throne,
A jealous rival piercing through me,
A nasty candidate is he.
My Silence? He replaced with yelling,
My laughter? Simply changed to fear,
My derby hat? He named a helmet,
The crowd won't even shed a tear,
He changed my song into a shriek,
He stole my mustache, stole my trick.
La, la, la, la, la, la.

When Bodo finished his song, he walked off stage like Charlie Chaplin. Laughter and applause filled the theater, and the curtain went down.

The next time the curtain went up, the talented Polish tenor, Jan Kiepura, sang an aria from Giacomo Pucini's opera, *Tosca*,' titled, "E Lucevan Le Stelle." The libretto to this opera was written by Luigi Illica and Giuseppe Giacosa.

Kiepura started singing:

E un passo sfiorava la rena
Entrava ella, fragrante,
Mi cadea fra le braccia
Oh! dolci baci, o languide carezze
Mentr'io fremente le belle forme discogliea dai veli!
Svanì per sempre il sogno mio d'amore.
L'ora e fuggita e muoio disperato!
E non ho amato mai tanto la vita!

English translation:

And the stars were shining
And the earth was smelling
The orchard gate creaked
And a footstep grazed the sand
She entered, fragrant
She fell into my arms.

When he finished the aria, Kiepura received tremendous applause. Bodo even came on stage and gestured for the audience to calm down. Then Bodo recited excerpts from Polish National Poet Slowacki, Juliusz's* drama, *Kordian.*

> Brothers! Poles! Brothers! Jews! Great thought is needed from heaven or earth! I took a look from the top. The knightly spirit has risen. Winkelried, Arnold von* took enemy spears and drove them into their hearts. People! Winkelried is back. Poland—the Winkelried of nations. She will sacrifice as she did many times in the past. Carry me clouds! Carry me winds! Carry me birds! For the last few centuries, Poland was covered by a sight of relentless cruelty of tyrants. Brothers! Poles!
> Jews! Another tyrant is approaching!

When Bodo finished, the subdued audience was silent and tearful. Then there was loud applause.

People who hadn't read Slowacki's *Kordian* had no idea who Winkelried was.

Ben Rosen promised Lacey and Mabel to tell them the story of Winkelried when they got home. When they left the theater, Ben invited Lacey, Frederick, Mabel, Adam, Esther, and Robert to his place, and after serving some French wine and snacks, he began telling them the story of Winkelried.

"I'm sure that Frederick already knows this story, right?" Ben started.

"I do," answered Frederick.

"You see, my dear friends, Poland is seething with history, but Austria and Switzerland have their own. Arnold von Winkelried was a Swiss hero. In 1386, he fought as an army soldier in the Old Swiss Confederacy in the Battle of Sempach against the Austrian army of Habsburg Duke Leopold III. On the day of the battle, the Austrian pikemen kept very close ranks, which could not be breached by the Swiss confederate forces. However, toward the end of the battle, the situation changed in favor of the Swiss. Why? Swiss soldier Arnold von Winkelried, who had a wife and children, sacrificed his life by throwing himself on the pikes of the Austrian pikemen and taking many of them down, a real Swiss hero," Ben ended the story.

Although Frederick was sitting next to Lacey, Ben looked at her like a man who was secretly in love.

Because the theme of history and culture came up so often lately, Ben Rosen decided to take Lacey and Mabel to visit Warsaw's Royal Castle to see an exhibit of Warsaw cityscapes painted by Venetian painter Bellotto, Bernard*. Belotto was the nephew and also a student of the world-famous Venetian painter Canal, Antonio*.

Canaletto, as he was more commonly-known, lived in the eighteenth century. His paintings are exhibited in almost every major museum and private collection in the world. During his stay in Warsaw, Bellotto lived at the Royal Castle where King Poniatowski, Stanislaw* resided. He died in Warsaw in 1780, having never returned to Venice.

As they walked through the exhibit, Lacey and Mabel were grateful that Ben brought them here to enjoy the beautiful paintings of Warsaw. While admiring Bellotto's great talent, they could feel themselves falling more in love with the Paris of the East.

September 1, 1939—Drama in the Paris of the East

It was March of 1939. Mabel went to visit her lover, Adam Czarny.

That same day, Ben Rosen and Lacey decided to take a walk near Castle Square past the granite and bronze statue of Sigismund's Column, which was erected in 1644. One of the most famous landmarks in Warsaw, it was also the first secular monument in the form of a column in modern history.

"The column and the statue commemorate King Sigismund Vasa III who moved Poland's capital from Krakow to Warsaw in 1596. The king is dressed in armor and carries a cross in one hand and wields a sword in the other," Ben explained.

"Incredible," Lacey said.

Castle Square was surrounded by many kawiarnias (cafes). Lacey loved the tantalizing aromas of fresh coffee and pastries.

Amfiteatr cafe served the best Napoleon pastries, Ziemianska coffee shop was famous for their delicious cream cakes, and Kultura cafe had the strongest coffee—everybody called it Satan.

Lacey never missed stopping at Blickle's pastry shop for paczki, tender moist donuts filled with plum filling. She absolutely loved the taste of them. Blickle's paczki was actually quite famous throughout Europe, and every morning, they were shipped to Paris.

March 31, 1939, *Kurier Warszawski* news: Neville Chamberlain, Prime Minister of England, best known for his foreign policy of appeasement and for signing the Munich Agreement, ceded Czechoslovakia's Sudetenland to Germany and gave a speech in the

House of Commons offering the British "guarantee" of Poland's independence.

April 4, 1939. The latest news from the *Kurier* informed that Polish Foreign Minister Colonel Jozef Beck signed a treaty in London designed to lateralize Neville Chamberlain's Polish Guarantee of March 31, which offered Poland protection from the Reich.

At the end of April, Henryk Wars, the composer, and Frederick stopped by to visit Ben Rosen at his apartment. And who else joined them? Well, no other than Professor Ludwik Hirszfeld. He stopped by to tell Ben some good news, that his daughter, Marysia, was returning to Poland during her school vacation. She was studying in Paris at the Sorbonne University. Ben Rosen was very happy about this visit because he'd been waiting to discuss the topic of Jewish geniuses with Professor Hirszfeld, Ludwik*, knowing he was one of them.

"So let's talk about gaons," Ben began.

"Gaons?" Frederick asked, not understanding what Ben was talking about.

"Gaon in Hebrew means genius," Henryk Wars explained.

"Aha," Frederick nodded.

"Only two Jewish geniuses were not born in Poland. Albert Einstein, one of the greatest physicists known for developing the theory of relativity, was born in Ulm, Germany, and Jonas Salk, who developed the first polio vaccine, was born in New York City. The others were all born in Poland," Ben ended proudly.

"Can you name them, please?" Frederick asked.

"Well, there's Professor Hirszfeld who is here with us. He was the first to prove that ABO blood group incompatibility between mother and fetus may cause damage to the newborn. He was born in Lodz. Then there's Sabin, Albert* who was born in Bialystok and developed the oral polio vaccine. Next there's the prominent Jewish physicist, Michelson, Albert*, who won the Nobel Prize for his invention of the Michelson interferometer. He was born in Strzelno. And finally, Rickover, Hyman*, the father of America's Nuclear Navy, especially submarines, was born in Maków Mazowiecki." Ben Rosen finished his brief history lesson, leaving his guests rapt with attention.

"Fascinating," said Frederick.

On September 1,1939, Nazi German planes began their aerial bombardment of Warsaw.

"This is very scary," Ben said to Lacey and Frederick.

All three were hiding in the basement of the building where Lacey and Mabel lived. They felt somewhat safe there as the buildings near Lazienki Park were solidly built and could withstand bombardments.

In the meantime, Mabel was staying at Adam Czarny's place near the Sluzewiec horse track outside Warsaw. They had a better chance of surviving the bombardment in the suburbs.

Under the international rules regarding aerial warfare in 1939, Warsaw was considered a legitimate military target as the city was on the front lines during the fighting, and it was heavily defended by the Polish army.

Despite German radio broadcasts claiming to have captured Warsaw, the initial attack was repelled, and soon, Warsaw was under the siege. Approximately 18,000 Varsovians perished during this siege. On September 3, Neville Chamberlain announced England's declaration of war on Germany.

The siege lasted until September 28, 1939, when the Polish garrison finally capitulated. The very next day, 140,000 Polish troops left the city and were taken as prisoners of war. As a result of the air bombardments, 10 percent of the city's buildings were destroyed.

After the bombing stopped, Ben, Lacey, and Frederick walked the street of Warsaw to see the general damage, and they noticed a group of people gawking at a man's body lying on the pavement. When Lacey looked closer, she noticed that it was the body of one of Warsaw's famous Black gentleman, the American Mr. Mississippi, who apparently was killed during the bombardment. His white hat lay next to his body.

Lacey noticed tears in Ben's eyes, but he quickly covered his face so she couldn't see. "God must see our tears," she said crying.

September 17, 1939. Checking a few kiosks around Warsaw, Ben Rosen and Frederick couldn't find the *Kurier Warszawski*, but they were able to find another newspaper, *Goniec Warszawski*. Frederick took a glimpse at the front page and couldn't believe what he was reading. The heading of the paper read: "The Soviet Union Invades Poland and Occupies Eastern Polish Territories."

"Incredible. Why are we so popular? Are we so rich that everyone wants a piece of us?" Frederick asked.

"It's not all about money. In Bialystok, on Poland's eastern border, my friends saw some Russians without socks. They were hungry and just wanted food. Remember, Polish farmers are still some of the best producers in Europe," Ben replied.

"Are they better producers than our German bauers?" Frederick asked unconvinced.

"I think the competition is very close. But speaking of gold, let me tell you what I heard from my friend who works at the Polish National Bank," Ben Rosen began. "Aside from the rich arrases (tapestries) of Krakow's Wawel Castle, gold is the most valuable Polish national treasure. The Polish National Bank in Warsaw made the decision to evacuate its gold reserves to the Bank of Lublin, the largest city on Poland's eastern border. On September 5, hundreds of bank employees armed with weapons used buses to move eighty tons of Polish gold to the Bank of Lublin. They preferred using buses over trucks so they could better camouflage the transfer," Ben finished.

"Incredible," Frederick said.

Ben could never have predicted what eventually happened with the gold. Nazi spies located the cache in Lublin. The bank decided to move the eighty tons of gold to Romania, so they worked for forty-eight hours straight to load the gold onto a tanker headed for a port in the Black Sea. From there, they reached Romania and then on to Istanbul in order to evade the diligent Nazis. Next, the Polish gold was transported by train to Beirut, Lebanon. By October, eighty tons of Polish gold arrived in the city of Nevers on the Loire River in central France where it was finally safe.

Ben continued, "Let me tell you another true story about my uncle who lives in the little town of Lowicz located ninety kilometers from Warsaw. My uncle works at the Lowicz Inn, but he also owns a small farm with a few sheep, one cow, and some hens and ducks. Because it was September, my uncle wanted to celebrate Rosh Hashanah, the Jewish New Year, so he slaughtered a sheep.

"Caravans of Nazi Wehrmacht soldiers wearing goggles and riding motorcycles were seen driving east on the roads outside of Lowicz. Why east, I asked? My uncle replied that Hitler always hated communists, and most likely, sooner or later, the German Wehrmacht will attack the Soviet Union.

"Because my uncle needed some help with his livestock, he found a good German man in Lowicz named Frantz. Frantz had worked at my uncle's farm for twelve years. It was an unusually hot day in September, so a group of German soldiers stopped at my uncle's farm for a drink of water. My uncle served them some cold water and everything initially seemed to be fine. They rested awhile, and then some soldiers started looking around the farm. One of the soldiers spotted some fresh blood from the slaughtered sheep near the barn. This soldier assumed that the blood must have been from a German soldier killed in passing. He quickly found a piece of rope, made a noose, and put it around my uncle's neck. He wanted to hang him on the spot.

"Seeing this, Frantz spotted a high-ranking Wehrmacht officer and begged him for my uncle's life. 'Bitte, bitte, ich bin unschuldig. Er ist ein guter mann,' Frantz begged in German, which meant 'Please, please, he is innocent. He is a good man.' Frantz also took the officer to the barn and showed him the slaughtered sheep. After seeing this, the Wehrmacht officer, being a reasonable person, released my uncle.

"In the morning, the Wehrmacht soldiers left, and my uncle started looking around for Frantz. He couldn't find him anywhere. He assumed that Frantz took the cow out to graze, so he went to the field to find him. And what did he discover? Next to the cow was Frantz's lifeless body. He was shot to death by the unforgiving, ruthless Nazis. Because the Wehrmacht officer didn't let them kill my uncle, they killed a good German man, Frantz, instead. He was one of their own blood, and the Nazis didn't care. They just wanted to demonstrate their power," Ben finished his story.

"Very sad to kill someone for no reason," Frederick commented sadly.

On October 1, the Wehrmacht Army soldiers entered Warsaw, starting the period of German occupation. The Wehrmacht soldiers were placed in the Warsaw Citadel. The Warsaw Citadel (in Polish, Cytadela Warszawska) is a nineteenth century fortress. It was built by the order of Tsar Nicholas I in order to bolster imperial Russian control of the city. It served as a prison well into the late 1930s.

The list of Poles imprisoned there included political activist Apollo Korzeniowski, father of the famous writer Joseph Conrad Korzeniowski, and Marshal of Poland Josef Pilsudski, who, in 1920, defeated the Bolsheviks during the Polish-Bolshevik War in the Battle of Warsaw.

The Nazis named Ludwig Fischer as their governor of Warsaw. His assistant was Kurt Schermann. Luckily, Frederick von Ulrich knew Kurt from his college years when he lived in Berlin. Frederick was surprised that Kurt joined the Nazi party because he was a homosexual, which was forbidden according to Nazi ideology. To propagate the Aryan master race, homosexuals were considered socially abhorrent, and the Nazis willingly condemned and persecuted them.

Ben Rosen, Adam Czarny, and Frederick von Ulrich met at Lacey and Mabel's apartment to discuss how to behave during the German occupation.

"Lacey and Mabel, how are you feeling? Are you scared? Being American citizens, you should be safe here, but under German occupation, your lives will be different now," Ben started the discussion around safety.

"These times are unprecedented. Downright unbelievable!" Frederick commented.

"Girls! Be extra careful. You can't assume how any Nazi might react at any moment, although there is a difference between any regular drafted Wehrmacht soldier and a soldier, who believed in Nazi ideology," Ben continued.

"Oh, there definitely is," Frederick added.

"Frederick, you too must watch yourself. You worked at the German Embassy in Warsaw during pre-Nazi times. You never know who you might run into. Renew your contacts in Berlin," Ben suggested.

"I'll try," said Frederick.

November 1939 passed quietly, but December was a very stressful month for Frederick. He was tasked with helping the Wehrmacht troops prepare for their first Christmas in Warsaw (Warschau in German).

When Governor Ludwig Fischer discovered that Frederick was once employed by the German Embassy in Warsaw, he sent his lieutenant to bring Frederick back to his office, pronto.

When the Nazi lieutenant showed up at Frederick's apartment and knocked on his door, he almost fainted out of fear. Frederick couldn't help but wonder why he was called to the governor's office. He dressed quickly and was escorted by the lieutenant to the Warsaw Citadel.

As he stepped out of the Nazi vehicle and saw the citadel decorated with large swastika banners, he was scared to enter the big doors.

Governor Fischer wanted to make the Wehrmacht troops happy, so he rented the Ateneum Theater to host a Christmas concert in German for all the troops. He even showed Frederick a list of names of performers he'd like to invite, including two famous German stars.

Governor Fischer made a suggestion to Frederick to join the Nazi party. Frederick refused, and the governor accepted his answer temporarily, but he promised to return to this subject. Looking at Governor Fischer's face showing disappointment, Frederick felt that he could be in trouble.

While talking to Frederick, Governor Fischer learned about two American singers in Warsaw who can sing in German. He suggested that maybe they could participate in this concert since Americans are known for being some of the best entertainers in show business.

Leaving the citadel, Frederick asked the Nazi lieutenant to drop him off at Lazienki Park, near Lacey and Mabel's apartment. Unsure of how Ben would react, Frederick was nervous asking the girls to participate in the concert.

He walked in, shouting, "Mabel! Lacey! Would you sing your greatest hit, 'Bei Mir Bist Du Schoen,' at the Wehrmacht Christmas concert? Please do it for me. Governor Fisher wouldn't take 'nein' for an answer. I'm scared of him. Would you sing the German version of the song for the troops?" Frederick asked, out of breath.

Ben Rosen was in the room but didn't say a word. Frederick knew that Ben wanted both girls to survive this ordeal. Ben finally agreed that it would be best for the girls to fulfill the governor's request to sing at the Christmas event and share their talents with the audience.

The day of the concert had finally arrived. At the theater, the girls took a peek from behind the curtain. The gray uniforms of the Wehrmacht Army soldiers in the audience intimidated both American stars. Before their performance, Ben Rosen reminded Lacy and Mabel not to accidentally sing the Yiddish version of the song. They didn't forget and sang "Bei Mir Bist Du Schoen" in German.

Their performance was beautiful, and the soldiers gave them a standing ovation while chanting "Sehr gut, sehr gut." Their cheers could even be heard outside the Ateneum Theater.

"Incredible," Frederick said, mumbling.

Hirszfeld, the Warsaw Ghetto, and the Departure

June 1940

After the occupation of Warsaw by the Wehrmacht Army, Hirszfeld was dismissed as a non-Aryan from the Hygiene Institute. He managed to do further work at home, but it was impossible for him to publish any of his findings.

In the 1940s, Hirszfeld was forced to move with his wife, Hanna, and daughter, Marysia, to the Warsaw Ghetto. In the ghetto, he organized campaigns against typhus and typhoid. Between March and June of 1940, he and his family fled the ghetto with the help of some Polish friends. They were able to survive using fake Polish names and documents. They had continually changed their addresses to stay safe. Sadly, his daughter, Marysia, died of tuberculosis later that year.

Some scientists from Germany continued to visit Hirszfeld in Warsaw, including Emil von Durgen from Heidelberg. He was grateful to Hirszfeld for saving his child when he was living in Berlin, but Hirszfeld modestly told him he owed it to German science.

Love was in the air at Lazienki Park. Adam Czarny loved Mabel. Frederick adored Lacey. Ben, however, continued to keep his love for Lacey a secret. All three men enjoyed spending time at Lacey and Mabel's place; they all felt comfortable and safe there.

"While speaking of Hirszfeld, you only mentioned Jewish geniuses. How about Polish ones?" Frederick asked.

Adam quickly chimed in, “Let’s see, there was Nicolaus Copernicus, the famous astronomer born in Torun in the fifteenth century who formulated a model that placed the sun at the center of our universe. Next, there’s Maria Skłodowska-Curie, born in Warsaw, who won the Nobel Prize for her research on radioactivity. Her daughter, Irene Curie also won a Nobel prize in chemistry. And don’t forget about the talented Polish writers like Henryk Sienkiewicz and Wladyslaw Reymont who won the Nobel Prize in literature.”

“Speaking of Polish talents, has anyone seen Henryk Wars lately?” Frederick asked.

“No. I haven’t seen him in a while,” Adam responded.

“Let me tell you what I heard yesterday about our talented composer. Last November, the movie *Ninotchka* was produced in Hollywood by Metro-Goldwyn-Mayer starring Greta Garbo and Melvyn Douglas. Who do you think wrote the screenplay for this movie? None other than Billy Wilder, who was born in Bielsko-Biala in southern Poland. In 1933, Billy Wilder went via Paris to Hollywood, and by 1939, he was already famous. Henryk Wars decided to follow in his footsteps and go to Hollywood. How is this possible in our crazy times? Maybe he also had some connections in Paris or maybe someone in the Polish underground helped him leave this hell on earth. Henryk Wars always said that he wanted to write music for Billy Wilder’s movies, and now, maybe, he can do it. He is a great composer. He wrote music for almost all of Bodo’s movies,” Ben Rosen finished.

Adam Czarny and Mabel decided to leave the company of their friends and go to dinner at the Bristol Hotel. When they sat down at their table, Mabel noticed a few German officers sitting nearby, looking at her and Adam and laughing. She just ignored them. And then she noticed August Agboola Browne, the percussionist from Nigeria, playing on the stage with the band.

August recognized Mabel right away from their time performing at Komedia. When the band stopped playing, he joined Mabel and Adam at their table. He was dressed very elegantly, even wearing a bowtie. After he ordered a glass of wine, he opened up about his current situation in Warsaw.

"When Komedia cabaret closed, I played at other restaurants around Warsaw until I finally found a job here at Bristol. When the war started, I began working for the resistance, distributing their newspapers and trading electronic equipment. I knew I had to join the Polish Underground to fight Nazis," August explained.

"Do you know what happened to Julien Scott?" Adam asked.

"He is still playing saxophone in restaurants around Warsaw as far as I know," August replied.

"It's getting harder and harder to survive these days in this hell," Adam said.

"I became a Nigerian-Polish resistance fighter after the Underground helped my wife and children leave Warsaw and go to England. Aside from being a percussionist at Bristol, I give private piano lessons to students at my home. I also shelter refugees from the Warsaw Ghetto. Contact me if you know someone who will need my help. Here is my address," August said.

"Frederick would say 'incredible!'" Mabel said, laughing.

"Thank you. We will remember your offer," Adam replied, squeezing Mabel's hand.

"And how is Frederick doing? Is he still with Lacey?" August asked.

"He is ready to go back to Berlin, but Lacey is keeping him here. However, Lacey is also very fond of Ben, so who knows what will happen," Mabel replied.

Apparently, some "friendly" soul ratted on Ben Rosen to Governor Fischer, and within a few hours, Ben was arrested and placed in the Warsaw Ghetto.

Lacey was heartbroken. At first, she wanted to file a complaint to the American Embassy, which is what any good law-abiding citizen would normally do if they were in the United States. However, she quickly realized that she was in Nazi-occupied Warsaw, so she instead went straight to Governor Fischer's office at the citadel and filed a complaint regarding Ben's arrest. She told the governor that Ben Rosen was innocent of any wrongdoing. Because Lacey was an American citizen and Governor Fischer respected her, he promised to look into Ben's case.

A few weeks had passed, and there was still no reply from the governor's office. Frederick promised Lacey that he would get Ben Rosen out of the ghetto. He remembered his old friend, Kurt Schwermann, and thought he was the only person in the office who could be bribed.

Because he was gay, Kurt would be in real danger if the Nazis found out about his sexual preference. Frederick chose Kurt to help him get Ben released from the ghetto. But there was a price to pay for doing so.

Frederick asked Lacey and Mabel to give him their diamond jewelry, which they happily agreed to do in order to save Ben. He also asked Lacey for the diamond earrings Aaron had given her, but she refused, and Frederick respected her decision.

Next, Frederick took the jewels to Kurt's office, placed them on his desk, and waited to see if this would be enough to close their deal. Kurt looked at the diamonds and quickly put them in his drawer. Frederick knew that Kurt could be bribed. He signed Ben's release from the ghetto on the spot and gave it to Frederick who quickly left Kurt's office.

Frederick raced to pick up Adam, and together, they went to the ghetto to find Ben. When they arrived at the ghetto's gate, Frederick was not under any suspicion from the guards because he spoke perfect German. However, Adam was still concerned about his own safety. When they crossed the ghetto's gate, they realized that they never really knew what true hell was. They looked around at the ghetto's inhabitants, worrying about what would later happen to these innocent people. The guards finally brought Ben who was very happy to see Frederick and Adam's friendly faces.

Adam remembered August Agboola Browne's words about sheltering refugees from the ghetto, but he had another idea about a hideout for Ben. He took Ben to his horse stables at Sluzewiec. Adam knew Ben would be safe there, and he wanted to make sure that Ben would never return to the ghetto.

Unfortunately, the Nazis worked diligently to find out who was behind Ben's release from the ghetto. They interrogated Kurt Schermann and learned about his deal with Frederick. The Nazis immediately arrested Frederick and brought him to the citadel. Shortly after, he was executed by firing squad for bribing a German official and helping a Jew escape from the ghetto.

Lacey was heartbroken after learning about Frederick's fate. She asked Adam to take her to the stables where Ben was hiding. Mabel was already there, and she greeted and consoled a very tearful Lacey.

"What a tragedy. Frederick was such a good man and German patriot," Lacey said, crying on Ben's shoulder.

"Remember the story about Frantz and my uncle in Lowicz? Wasn't I correct to say that Nazis are bloodthirsty and ruthless people? They killed Frederick, one of their own," said Ben.

Ben could still hear Frederick quoting one of his favorite authors: "People who don't submit to God today will submit to tyrants tomorrow."

"Did he tell you this writer's name?" asked Adam.

"Unfortunately, I never asked," Ben replied.

*****

Back in New York, Aaron was closely monitoring the situation in Warsaw to stay informed about Lacey and Mabel's whereabouts. They were now staying at Adam Czarny's place at the Służewiec race track because it was safer there. However, it was becoming more and more difficult to survive in Warsaw, especially with Ben hiding in one of the horse stables. Both Mabel and Lacey were waiting for any chance to leave the city.

The Nigerian-Polish underground in Warsaw was organizing night flight missions out of Warsaw via LOT Polish Airlines. One day, August Agboola Browne stopped by Adam's place to inform him of a special night flight mission to Beirut. LOT was still able to use tarmacs outside of Warsaw during the German occupation.

"If you want to leave, meet me tomorrow at midnight on the tarmac," August suggested.

"We'll do it. There is no time to wait. We'll take the Beirut flight," Adam replied.

Adam told everybody to get their documents and pack a few things, just the necessities. He called some friends to make arrangements for his horses, his first love. He was now ready to go anywhere with his second love, Mabel.

All four—Lacey Starr, Mabel Brown, Ben Rosen, and Adam Czarny—arrived at the tarmac at midnight. They quickly boarded the plane, and even though they were scared of the unknown, they felt some relief to finally be on the move. They stayed in Beirut for almost a week. They wanted to stay longer, but Aaron informed Lacey that Ignatzio was dead, and they were safe to return home. They decided to fly to London and from there take a transatlantic ocean liner back to New York.

Shortly after their departure for New York, the Nigerian-Polish underground fighter, August Agboola Browne, also fled Poland; he was able to board a night mission flight to London where he joined his wife and sons.

When Lacey, Mabel, Ben, and Adam arrived in New York, Aaron Glickman greeted them at the harbor's terminal.

"I'm so happy that your journey is over and that you made it back home safely," Aaron said, hugging both Lacey and Mabel.

There was no end to the hugging and kissing that ensued; everyone was so happy to finally be together. Aaron was already good friends with Lacey, Mabel, and Ben, but he had never met Adam Czarny. He had only heard stories about Adam from Ben and was happy to finally meet the person responsible for saving Ben's life. The whole group was so happy to finally be safe and among friends.

"Welcome to America. It seems to me that these two gentlemen, Ben and Adam, will become great American citizens in the future," Aaron said.

"We'll never be apart," Adam said, putting his arms around Mabel.

"We won't either, Ben. Am I right?" Lacey asked.

"Lacey, I've wanted to tell you that I love you since we lived in Warsaw, but I never had the chance," Ben said, looking into Lacey's beautiful eyes.

Lacey blushed and was smiling from ear to ear.

"Oh yes! Warsaw will not be the same without you guys," said Aaron, laughing.

"I still love Warsaw because it's my home, but now I'm ready to explore New York. From what I've heard, I will love this beautiful city as well," Ben replied.

"Me too," said Adam.

After a couple of days of getting settled in New York, Aaron invited Lacey, Mabel, and his two new guests from Poland to a classy night club. Since the 200 Club was long gone. This was the next best place.

Aaron had a little surprise for Lacey. He had arranged with the stage manager of the club for Lacey to sing. She couldn't believe he asked her to get on stage and sing to the sizable audience gathered in the club. Aaron exchanged a couple words with the stage manager and joined Mabel, Ben, and Adam at their table. Lacey sang the Frank Sinatra hit "I'll Never Smile Again" with music by Ruth Love and lyrics by Ruth Love and Tommy Dorsey. When Lacey looked at Ben Rosen, you could see the love in her eyes as she started to sing:

I'll never smile again
Until I smile at you,
I'll never smile again
What good would it do?
For tears would fill my eyes
My heart would realize
That our romance is through
I'll never love again
I'm so in love with you
I know I will never start
To smile again
Until I smile at you.

Lacey finished singing and kept looking at Ben, her love. The audience applauded because she sang so beautifully and sincerely that you really could feel the love in the air.

“Incredible,” said Adam, sitting at the table with his arms around Mabel.

They looked at each other and smiled, remembering Frederick; it was his favorite word after all. The incredible journey of Lacey Starr and Mabel Brown had finally come to a conclusion. Or was this just the beginning?

Lacey Starr and Ben Rosen got married and had two sons, Aaron and Frederick, named after Aaron Glickman and Frederick von Ulrich who gave his life to save Ben Rosen from the Warsaw Ghetto. Adam Czarny married Mabel Brown, and they had two daughters, Jezebel and Marysia, named after Hirszfeld’s daughter who died of tuberculosis back in Poland.

Appendix

Polish-Bolshevik War (1920–1921)—Conflict between Soviet Russia and the Second Polish Republic with decisive Polish victory at the Battle of Warsaw. (Page 13, 24, 64)

Cooper, Merian (1903–1973)—A member of the American Flight Squadron, which supported the Polish Army in the Polish-Bolshevik War. His plane was shot down, and he spent nine months in a Soviet POW camp. He escaped, and for his valor, he was honored with the highest military order, the Virtuti Militari. (Page 13)

Fauntleroy, Cedric (1891–1973)—Colonel in the American Air Force, who in 1920 volunteered to serve in the Polish Air Force during Polish-Bolshevik War. He made four hundred flights against Soviet Forces. His honors were Silver Cross of Virtuti Militari and Cross of Valour (four times). (Page 13)

Battle of Warsaw—Known as the Miracle on the Vistula River which was a series of battles that resulted in a decisive Polish victory in 1920 over the Red Army. (Page 14, 64)

Mustafa, Kara, Pasha (1634–1683)—Ottoman nobleman, Grand Vizier, military figure, attempted expansion into Central Europe. (Page 14)

Sobieski, Jan (1629–1696)—King of Poland, famous for his victory over the Ottoman Empire at the Battle of Vienna in 1683, known as the "Lion of Lechistan." (Page 14)

Husaria—Polish Hussars known as the winged Hussars, heavy cavalry formation used in the Kingdom of Poland from 1503 to 1702. (Page 14)

The Black Madonna (Our Lady of Czestochowa)—Miraculous image of the Immaculate Conception, the Blessed Virgin Mary in the Clear Mountain. Painted by St. Luke, brought to Poland in the fourteenth century, the image became the national symbol of Poland. (Page 15)

Sienkiewicz, Henryk (1846–1910)—Polish historical novelist. He traveled to the US in the late 1870s. His books are as follows: *With Fire and Sword*, *The Deluge*, *Sir Michael*, and *Quo Vadis*. (Page 16, 68)

Byzantium—An ancient Greek city, founded in the seventh century BC. It was rebuilt by Constantine the Great in AD 324 as Constantinople. (Page 17)

King Casimir the Great (1310–1370)—King of Poland. He ended a thirteen-year war against the Teutonic Knights in his favor. He improved conditions of Jews, encouraged industry, commerce and agriculture, founded the Jagiellonian University in Krakow in 1364. (Page 18)

Teutonic Knights—The Teutonic Order (German: Deutscher Orden) is a Catholic religious order founded as a military order in 1190 in Acre, Kingdom of Jerusalem. Between 1701 and 1918, they stayed in the Kingdom of Prussia, now Poland. (Page 18)

Lodz—The third largest city in Poland and a former industrial center. (Pages 18, 51, 60)

Bodo, Eugeniusz (1899–1943)—A skilled singer. He became an icon of Polish musical comedy and a symbol of Polish commercial cinema of the late 1930s born in Switzerland. (Page 26)

Jolson, Al (1886–1950)—An American singer, comedian, actor, and vaudevillian. He was referred to by critics as "the king of black-face performers." (Page 26)

Chaney, Lon (1883–1930)—An American actor, director, screen-writer. One of the most versatile and powerful actors of cinema.

Ordonowna, Hanka (1902–1950)—Polish singer, dancer, and actress. (Page 26, 29)

Wars, Henryk (born Henryk Warszawski) (1902–1977)—A Polish composer. He composed scores to fifty movies in Poland in 1930s and sixty more in the United States. (Page 26, 30, 31, 33, 34, 37, 44, 60, 68)

Tuwim, Julian (1894–1987)—A Polish poet, a major figure in Polish literature. (Page 26, 55)

Negri, Pola (1897–1953) (born in Apolonia Chalupiec)—A Polish stage and film actress. She achieved worldwide fame during the silent and golden eras of Hollywood movies. (Page 27)

The Fuhrer—Adolf Hitler (1889–1945)—An Austrian born chan-cellor of Germany, leader of Nazi party. (Page 35)

The Reichstag—The German Parliament building in Berlin. (Page 35)

Ben-Gurion, David (1886–1973) (born as David Grun in Plonsk, Poland)—He was the leader of the Jewish community in Palestine. Subsequently he became known as "Israel's Father," first prime minister of Israel 1948–1954. (Page 46)

Kiepura, Jan (1902–1966)—A Polish singer (tenor) and actor. (Page 55, 56)

Slowacki, Juliusz (1809–1849)—A Polish National and Romantic poet. His best works include dramas "Kordian" and "Balladyna" and poems "Beniowski," "My Testament," and "Anhelli." (Page 57)

Winkelried, Arnold, von—A legendary hero in Swiss history. (Page 57, 58)

Bellotto, Bernardo (1721–1780)—Urban landscape painter. He was the student and nephew of the renowned Giovanni Antonio Canal Canaletto. (Page 58)

Canal, Antonio Giovanni (1697–1768)—Commonly known as Canaletto, Italian painter From Venice, known as genius Canaletto. (Page 58)

Poniatowski, Stanislaw August (1732–1798)—King of Poland and Grand Duke of Lithuania from 1764 to 1795. (Page 58)

Hirszfeld, Ludwik (1884–1954)—Polish-Jewish microbiologist and serologist. (Page 38, 49, 50, 51, 52, 60, 67, 74)

Sabin, Albert—Jewish doctor, developed the oral Polio vaccine, born in Bialystok, Poland. (Page 60)

Michelson, Albert—American-Jewish physicist born in Strzelno, Poland, won Nobel Prize in science in 1907 for the Michelson Interferometer. (Page 60)

Rickover, Hyman (1900–1986)—An American-Jewish admiral who directed the original development of naval nuclear propulsion. He was born in Maków Mazowiecki, Poland. (Page 60)

About the Author

Perry Dantes aka Perry Nowakowski was born in Aleksandrów Kujawski, Poland. He attended Nicolas Copernicus University in Poland and the University of Wisconsin-Milwaukee.

CPSIA information can be obtained
at www.ICGtesting.com
Printed in the USA
LVHW030444061222
734629LV00006B/260

9 781684 985760